（汉英）

命運好好玩

蔡瀾 作品

CNS PUBLISHING & MEDIA
湖南文艺出版社 HUNAN LITERATURE AND ART PUBLISHING HOUSE
博集天卷 CS-BOOKY

在我四十岁那年，我感到我的生命正在消逝，
我知道我必须做些事情。

这世界没有奇迹，但佛像的神态，深深地刻在我脑海里。

当你旅行时，你会学到很多哲理。

目录

Contents

在玩乐中体验人生

生活充实，人就有信心

后记

English Version

Contents

I Choose to Live Fun

Experience Life While Having Fun

Life Is Full, People Have Confidence

POSTSCRIPT

我决定活得有趣

感谢这段时光

“文化大革命”时期，有一个男人经过池塘，看到水里有些浮萍。他带了几株回家，放在茶杯里用水养着。苦难的日子一天一天过着，那个男人每天看着浮萍慢慢繁盛，自得其乐。他的妻子对他的爱，也像浮萍一样与日俱增。

人生中总有些事想做，但往往没时间去做。当我们被隔离的时候，却因此得到了更多属于自己的时间。就趁这段时光，做一些想做又没时间做的事吧！如果我们一天天无所事事地度过，就等于输给了病毒。如果我们像那个种浮萍的男人一样，每天自得其乐，就是战胜了苦难。

一点不起眼的泡菜，就能让你的食物变成佳肴。将蔬菜的芯部切成你喜欢的形状，再用盐给它们按摩，然后静置一阵子，之后用厨房纸将水分吸干，再把它们放进玻璃罐子，加入半罐子白醋和半罐子凉白开（没煮开的水里面有微生物，会毁掉整罐泡菜）。加一点点糖，然后把盖子关紧，整罐翻过来放。一两天之后，泡菜就完成了。如果你喜欢吃咸的，就放点鱼露来代替白醋，鱼露在很多超市都能买到，也可以加入大蒜、辣椒和一点点白糖。根据自己的喜好来调味，找到一种适合自己口味的泡菜，会让你一吃就停不下来。

也可以尝试自己做冰淇淋。其实，做冰淇淋根本不需要昂贵的机器，两个密封袋足矣。冰淇淋并没有想象中那么难做，只需要冰和奶油。将浓缩奶油放进小的密封袋，然后把碎冰块和海盐装进大的密封袋。将小袋子装进大袋子里，把两个袋子里的原材料摇晃，直到混为一体，就是冰淇淋了。如果有不明白的，网上随时可以找到教学视频。

将自己的履历写下来，并生成一个二维码，放到自己的社交媒体，以后就可以节省介绍自己的时间。

把自己喜欢的歌曲组成歌单，分享给同好。

写电邮给老朋友，把以往的合影发给对方。

总有几百样想学的东西没学到，趁现在学。

总有几千件想做的事情没时间做，趁现在做。

而我，趁着这段时间，写了这本英文书，献给我那些不会中文的朋友。

希望你们喜欢。

意大利文名字

我的名字蔡澜，无论用潮汕话还是普通话，都很难让我说西班牙语的同事记住。有一天，他们集合起来跟我说："我们决定以后叫你马里奥（Mario）。"

我马上抗议："我们在西班牙，你们可以叫我何塞（Jose）、莱昂纳多（Leonardo）或者哈维尔（Javier）这些西班牙名字！为什么给我一个意大利名字？"

他们异口同声地说："因为你好吃得像个意大利人！"

大玩具

作为电影监制的最大乐趣，就是把电影当成一件大玩具。

在我刚到香港的时候，传统妓院（也就是"青楼"）已经被封禁。我在很多长辈的口中，听过不少关于香港石塘咀青楼的趣事，令人向往。那时候，我就决定制作一部关于青楼的电影，名叫《群莺乱舞》。

导演区丁平是我亲自挑选的。他原本是一位电影美术指导，他做事巨细无遗，在电影开拍之前，他把所有相关资料都研究个透，并在嘉禾影城里搭建了整个青楼的场景。

我们搜集了一席二十道菜的青楼菜谱，细心地将之重新设计并重现在观众眼前，当中还有几瓶年代久远的轩尼诗白兰地。这部电影选了当时最漂亮的女演员来主演（包括：关之琳、利智、刘嘉玲等），为这些女士设计长衫，对我来说是极大的乐趣。

戏中一位有钱的嫖客，我邀请了好朋友倪匡来出演。当时倪匡已经成名，经常出现在不同的电视节目中，也在报章、杂志写专栏。

这场戏将会拍摄一整晚，当我看到一切准备就绪，我便回家了。

当晚半夜，我的电话响起来了。

“倪先生喝光了四瓶白兰地，现在不省人事了！我该怎么办？”导演区丁平焦急地求救。

“你以前没看到过嫖客喝醉吗？”我冷静地回答他。

沉默片刻，区丁平如释重负地说：“我知道怎么拍了。”

倪匡被一群女孩逗弄取笑，成为这部电影经典的一幕。

厨房危机

在巴塞罗那拍电影的时候，成龙、洪金宝和我住在一栋带有独立厨房的公寓。当我们不需要拍摄的时候，我们就会做饭，做饭，做饭。

有一天，洪金宝家的厨房没有辣椒了，洪金宝便让他太太向我要一点。

我便抓了一把哈瓦那辣椒给她。

洪金宝看到辣椒后，轻蔑地说："蔡澜这家伙真小气，给我干干瘪瘪的辣椒！"他不知道，这是世界上最辣的一种辣椒。

当他切完辣椒，电话就响起来，他来不及洗手就去接电话，然后和朋友聊了一会儿。聊完之后他顺便上了个厕所。

小金宝连续肿了三天。

料理铁人

《料理铁人》曾是20世纪90年代日本最穷奢极欲的烹饪节目。当时日本经济繁荣，一集《料理铁人》的食菜费用就高达七百一十一万美金！这个节目非常成功，连续拍摄了七年，而且持续影响着整个世界的烹饪节目，直到今天。

来自全球的名厨，包括阿兰·帕萨德（Alain Passard）和皮埃尔·加涅尔（Pierre Gagnaire）都被吸引到《料理铁人》里，与日本的"铁厨"们每周比拼厨艺。节目组欣赏我对食材的认识，邀请我担任客席裁判。我答应了他们，因为他们也答应让我畅所欲言。其他裁判点评起来，都比较客气，只有我是例外。所以日本人给我取了一个花名——辛口，用现在的网络词汇来说，就是“毒舌”。

当最佳“铁厨”道场六三郎向我呈献一份龙虾的时候，我对他说：“把它拿走，这龙虾太硬了。”

他深深地向我鞠了一躬，并接受了我的点评，说：“是的，我煮过头了。”

现场观众齐声欢呼，他们已经对客气的点评感到厌烦，所以他们爱听我的点评。

我应邀出席了很多次，在节目当中，我开始留意到裁判团并不是每次都公平。

节目里总共有三位裁判，其中两名是日本人。他们与电视台沆瀣一气，因为他们觉得如果日本“铁厨”经常落败，会让他们丢了面子，所以那两位日本裁判总给日本“铁厨”高分，让他们击败挑战者。

这件事让我觉得很恶心，所以我制定了计划来对抗他们。

每次评分的满分是十分。两位日本裁判因为骨子里的客气，评分不会太极端，经常会给日本“铁厨”八分，给挑战者五分或六分。如果我觉得挑战者烹调得比较好，我会直接给挑战者十分，给“铁厨”零分，这让我欣赏的挑战者的平均分数比日本“铁厨”高。这个方法成功数次。后来电视台变聪明了，把裁判团的人数增加到四人或五人。我渐渐对这个节目失去了兴趣，并从此不再出席。

值得庆幸的是，作为客席裁判出现在这个节目上，为我打开了日本最好的各家餐厅的大门。就算是世界知名的Nobu餐厅，在我没有预订的情况下进入他们位于纽约翠贝卡（TriBeCa）区的餐厅，也把我当成贵宾招待。几年之后，我离开了电影行业，我与一群美食爱好者吃遍全球，我总能在日本最好的餐厅为大家预订到位置。

不久之前发生了另一件趣事。我突然收到一大笔肖像权使用费。

原来，有一家弹珠机公司用了《料理铁人》的节目内容来设计弹珠游戏，他们将最难进的洞口命名为“辛口”！

佛像

很多年前，我根据中国传统小说《水浒传》监制了一部电影。其中一幕就是武松打虎。我们做了一些研究，并在泰国找到了一只老虎。这只老虎客串过很多泰国电影，在当地已经算是明星了。我们到了当地的丛林，丛林里有一座在山上的庙。

周围村落的孩子都慕名来看它。这老虎看起来很友善。

我问：“它喜欢小朋友吗？”

“当然，”驯兽师顿了一顿，接着幽默地说，“为了食物。”

现场一切准备就绪，随时可以开始拍摄。

突然之间，天上乌云密布，狂风大作。录像机也失灵了，老虎更兽性大发。一切都变得一团糟。我们无奈地停止拍摄，我也开始慌乱。我无能为力，只急得团团乱转。当地的制作经理看到我焦急的模样，便对我说："这里是佛门圣地，当你来到这里工作，为什么不去庙里参拜一下？"

这时的我无计可施，参拜似乎是个好主意。我带着供品爬到山上，眼前出现了一座我有生以来看到过的最小的寺庙。佛像是用石头雕的。寺庙的天花板被风吹走了，佛像每天经历风吹雨打。佛像的面容和神态已经被侵蚀得模糊。一般来说，信众都会为佛像镀上金箔，但这座没有。这里香火一定稀疏，没有人前来供奉。

我跪在佛像前面，并开始讨价还价："我不是佛教徒，也不信神。我来这里，只求电影拍摄顺利。如果真的有神，请在十分钟内给我点启示，否则我就离开，不在这里浪费时间。"

十分钟过去了。我也清醒了。

这世界没有奇迹，但佛像的神态，深深地刻在我脑海里。

我对佛像深深作躬，然后就回到拍摄现场。

导演在怒吼，工作人员围着我，不停地问："现在怎么办？现在怎么办？"

我默不作声，只是面无表情地看着他们，跟那佛像一样。所有人渐渐冷静下来。之后，奇迹发生，天空开始放晴，老虎变得温顺，录像机突然又复原了。我们顺利地把这场戏拍好，再也没有遇到任何麻烦。

我们沿着山路离开的时候，再次经过那座破庙。一道阳光洒在了佛像之上，我仿佛看到他在微笑。

流言

李小龙真的死在丁佩家里。李小龙的尸体也真的在她床上。但还有很多流言并未证实。关于李小龙的死，有一个故事，大家比较少听到。

当警察到达现场的时候，已经有一大堆记者聚集。他们看到李小龙的尸体被床单盖着，抬了出去。所有人都冲过去，大吼着问："李小龙是不是真的中风死的？"

医护人员没有留下答案，把救护车开走了。

理所当然地，记者和摄影师也马上开车跟上。到了地方，护工把李小龙的尸体搬到床上，推进了停尸间，然后把门关上。

几个小时过去，记者和摄影师等得不耐烦了。

这时，有一个不修边幅的男人从停尸间开门出来抽烟。

"李小龙死的时候，下体是否仍然勃起？"这是当时现场所有人最想证实的流言。

"真的。"那人说。

“哇！”所有人都激动起来。

他们开始央求那个不修边幅的男人，让他们进去拍照。

那个不修边幅的护工说：“那得付钱。”

“多少钱？多少钱？”其他人此起彼落地问价。

“五百块。”

在20世纪70年代早期，五百块港币是一个大数目，他们开始犹豫。

那护工准备转身离开。

“等一下！等一下！”那些记者大声说，“至少你要给我们看一眼，我们才能跟老板申请啊！”

护工抓了抓头发，不情愿地点了点头。

他选了其中一个记者作为代表，护工把门开了一条缝，让记者代表瞄了一眼。

床单下面真的有东西一柱擎天！

记者代表回去跟其他同行确认了这件事。

当时没有手机，所有人都到电话亭排队，打电话向编辑汇报。这么大的一单新闻，所有编辑当然都会同意那五百元的费用。

于是他们轮流把钱交给护工，护工便指挥着他们说：“一个一个来！”

所有人都争取机会第一时间拍到照片，没有人理那个护工的话，大家都争先恐后挤进门里，停尸间一片混乱。

那护工已经阻止不了他们。

门被这群记者完全挤开，一阵强风也因此吹了进去。

那张床单也被强风吹到了半空。

床上垂直摆放着两个枕头，两个枕头中间，夹着一双筷子！

这里根本没有李小龙的尸体，更没有勃起！

在场的所有人，只想拿回他们的五百块，但那个护工已经不知所踪。

范·克里夫的假发

20世纪70年代，邵氏兄弟为了打开海外市场，制作了很多与外国电影公司的合拍电影，我一直参与其中。

最开始合作的是悍马电影（Hammer Films），一家专门制作恐怖片的英国电影公司。我小时候就看过他们的“德古拉伯爵”系列电影，这系列的每一部，我都喜欢。

当我知道我最喜欢的演员彼得·库欣（Peter Cushing）会来到我们的片场，拍摄《七金尸》，我非常高兴。

彼得是一个身材高挑、沉默寡言的人。

“库欣先生，为什么你总是那么严肃？”我问。

“谁会觉得一个僵尸杀手老是笑？”他开玩笑地回复，“作为一个演员我要身临其境。”

当时还有很多其他演员。我很记得李·范·克里夫（Lee Van Cleef），当时他来拍摄*Blood Money*，一部西方功夫电影，在美国名为《龙虎走天涯》（*The Stranger and the Gunfighter*）。

李当年才四十九岁，但看起来却很老。他已经有点地中海式脱发，只剩下头顶周围的一圈头发。他杯不离手，伏特加一瓶接着一瓶地喝。即使在拍摄的时候，他也是醉的。

他有一个私人定制的假发。这块圆形的假发，无论从哪个角度看，长短面积都是一样的。当导演让他准备拍摄，他只需把假发随便粘在头顶就可以了。他看着我，笑着说："很方便吧？"

的确方便。

洛曼历险记

20世纪70年代，灾难电影风靡一时。邵氏兄弟也与好莱坞合作，赶上这股热潮。

第一步是选导演，选择的是罗纳德·尼姆（Ronald Neame），他凭着《波塞冬历险》的成功，开创了灾难片的新时代。我们的演员阵容则有肖恩·康纳利（Sean Connery）和娜塔莉·伍德（Natalie Wood）主演，还有卡尔·莫尔登（Karl Malden）、特雷弗·霍华德（Trevor Howard）和亨利·方达（Henry Fonda）参演，这电影怎么可能失败？

可是，这部灾难片的结局就是票房上的灾难。

无论如何，我们在制作的过程中已经乐在其中。这部电影有一部分在香港拍摄，当时我负责监制这部分。

尼姆导演非常绅士，比较寡言。电影的摄影师保罗·洛曼（Paul Lohmann）则非常健谈，所以我和他成了朋友。我从他身上学到了很多使用灯光的知识，例如：

“当天气突然变差，开始下雨，我们是不是要停止拍摄？”

“不，不。我们可以利用灯光来拍摄特写镜头。”

“那你怎样让阴天变成晴天？”

“将九只一万瓦特的大灯并排，照向同一方向，就可以模拟阳光。”

“你是怎样判断什么时候需要用灯？”

“当你在室内，觉得房间的灯管比外面的阳光更亮的时候。”

我们在不用拍摄的时候，经常一起买醉。

“为什么你的脾气总是那么差，保罗？”

“因为我的儿子。他是一个好孩子，但却染上毒瘾。我经常因为自己没有时间陪伴他而生气。”

“那你可以为他做些什么吗？”

“有的。我尽我所能地陪伴他。”

“你有试过冥想吗？这是一个佛教的方法，能让你自然地获得快感。”

我教了他简单的方法。第二天，他告诉我冥想对他有用，他回家之后会与他儿子一起尝试。

从此之后我没再见过保罗。希望他一切顺利。

一种叫作“电影导演”的怪物

在我四十年的电影工作生涯，我遇到过无数导演。他们每一个都是怪物。

以前，导演的形象是挂着墨镜，戴着贝雷帽。一整天抽着大雪茄，身旁总有一个对讲机，坐在一张凳子上，背后写着“导演”二字。之后，导演的形象变成长发嬉皮士，穿着牛仔裤，形象一点都不权威。但他们都有一个共同点，就是为达目的不择手段，他们可以牺牲任何人，甚至是亲妈。

怎样成为一个导演？有些是红裤子出身[①]，有些是正统电影学院毕业，更有些是凭着他们的个人专长成为导演。当功夫片最流行的时候，连龙虎武师都有机会成为导演。曾经有一位台湾导演，当

① 从底层的场工、剧务做起，有丰富的基层经验。——编者注

日本摄影师告诉他拍摄当天差了点“色温”，那位导演就大发脾气。“色温”是靠光源来调节的。蜡烛可以带来偏暖、偏红的光，正午的阳光则会带来偏冷、偏蓝的光。那时候天仍亮着，那位龙虎武师出身的导演不明白为什么摄影师不能拍摄。他以为这是灯光设备所引起的问题，便转向制作经理，命令他说：“明天你多带点‘色温’！”

传统的导演最喜欢大喊“NG！”，意思就是“No Good！”。当他们走进摄影棚，导演为了显示他的权威，即使演员的演技很好，也会刻意地喊“NG”。拍摄外景时，如果天气不好，他会下令停止拍摄。不过，就算天气再好，他也会停止拍摄。一个年轻的助理无奈地问道：“为什么？”

“云的位置不对，你这傻子！”导演怒骂助手。

年轻的导演们会用双手制作一个无形的方框，并在他们走进演播室的那一刻大喊：“从这里拍摄！”老派的欧洲导演习惯一镜到底，称作“大师镜头”。从那里你开始越来越紧地拍摄，将它们编号为 1，3，5，7，9。一侧的拍摄完成后，你从另一侧拍摄时修改了角度，并将它们编号为 2，4，6，8，10。

由于缺乏经验，年轻的导演经常会忘记拍 3 或 8，然后一切都要重新开始，这时候摄制组就骂声震天，“满地爹娘”。

工作室制度也有一些好处。我们这些监制，在导演前面看到了样片。样片是电影未经处理和剪辑的版本，将不同镜头拍摄的影片拼接在一起，并不按顺序。

经验丰富的制片人可以看看这个故事是否讲得妥当，并会命令导演补拍。

举个例子：一个反派被警察追捕，他爬山逃生，跌倒身亡。

1. 反派爬上来的全镜头。

2. 他用假人摔倒的全貌。

3. 他死了的镜头特写。

我们会要求导演添加一个反派脚踩松动的石头的特写，然后是他尖叫的特写——“啊！”，这是让场景变得生动起来的方式。

一些新生代导演的问题是他们很少读书。他们从其他电影中吸收了一些片段，这使他们的电影成为二手的。这就是为什么你厌倦了所有这些特效电影。艺术电影可能很无聊，但它们有自己的观众。如果你决定制作它们，你必须了解它们的局限性。不能指望把一部艺术电影拍成票房大片。我总是向导演解释这一点，但他们从不听。

我在邵氏的时候，我们一年拍四十部电影。当时作为一个热血的年轻电影爱好者，我问老板邵逸夫：“如果我们一年拍四十部电影都赚钱，我们就不能拍一部有艺术感但会亏钱的电影吗？”

他笑着回答：“如果我们拍了三十九部赚钱的电影，一部不赚钱的电影，为什么不拍四十部都赚钱的电影？”

“作为电影制片人，你没有艺术良心吗？”香港影评人问我。我笑着回答：“我是有良心的。我的良心是为电影业的投资者赚钱。”

与托尼·柯蒂斯见面

“托尼·柯蒂斯（Tony Curtis）来了香港。要跟他见一面吗？”我的好朋友，香港美联社社长鲍勃·刘打电话给我。

“当然！”我说，我看过他所有的电影。

明星就是明星。他穿着一件短而紧的斗牛士外套。粉丝们立刻认出了他，他们要了他的签名，他欣然应允。

他那双锐利的蓝眼睛，看起来一点也不像七十九岁。

托尼头上是灰色的短发。

“我想念你以前的发型，”我直接说，“我曾经模仿过。”

“你并不是唯一的一个！我自己也尝试模仿。”托尼大笑着说。

“来香港是做什么的？”

“从电影中退休后，我开始绘画。我准备在伦敦办一场画展。我顺道在香港做几件西装。他们可以在24小时内完成！”

我注意到托尼一直拉着他的紧身夹克盖住他越来越大的肚子，但盯着他看是不礼貌的。我也对他的六个妻子很好奇，但这太私人了。

“你能告诉我，你与斯坦利·库布里克（Stanley Kubrick）合作的经历吗？”

“啊！他是最伟大的。他了解电影的一切，甚至在哪个镇的哪个剧院最适合放映他的电影。其他导演会把摄像机放在最引人注目的位置，但斯坦利却没有。他总是把摄像机放在最不起眼的角落，让演员感到安心。”

“电影放映时，《斯巴达克斯》中有一个场景被剪掉了。”我说。

“是的，”他说起这件事很兴奋，“我扮演了一个年轻的奴隶，为劳伦斯·奥利弗（Laurence Olivier）扮演的主人服务。当我为他刷背时，他正在吃蜗牛。他转过身来看着我说：‘有的喜欢蜗牛，有的喜欢牡蛎，我两个都喜欢。’这一场戏在20世纪60年代，是非常大胆的。斯坦利当时敢于处理同性恋，而且他做得很优雅。”

“劳伦斯·奥利弗呢？他是什么样的人？”

“当然是顶级的演员。很细心。每一个动作都像机器般精密。不过与他共事并不有趣。”他说。

“你是意大利人吗？”我转移了话题。

“每个人都以为是，其实我来自匈牙利。”

“你曾回去吗？”

“当它还是一个共产主义国家的时候曾回去。没什么值得说的。”

“你曾在第二次世界大战中服役。”我又换了个话题。

“是的，”他很高兴我知道这件事，“我在美国海军潜艇服役，挤在潜艇狭窄的走廊里，不是很舒服。所以我退役了。”

“你怎么能在战争中退出？”

“也许是因为我长得好看，”他开玩笑地说道，“他们让我光荣退伍，哈哈！”

“刚开始的演员生活是怎样的？”

“还挺顺利的。正如保罗·纽曼（Paul Newman）曾经说过的那样，在工作室制度下工作，就像去办公室一样。我们工作，然后吃午饭，然后继续工作，然后吃晚饭，喝得酩酊大醉，然后睡觉。”

“你还喝酒吗？”

“不了。我也不吃红肉。现在主要吃鸡肉。”

但我们让他破戒了。鲍勃和我一杯接一杯地喝着干马天尼。托尼被诱惑了，为自己点了一杯伏特加。

“死就死吧。”他说。

喝了几杯之后，托尼的表演欲变得强烈。他开始用叉子、香烟和餐巾变魔术。

“这个魔术来自Houdini（电影特效软件）。”

明星总需要观众。

“我们拍摄的每一部电影，工作室都请各行各业顶级专业人士来教我们。我们和伯特·兰卡斯特（Burt Lancaster）一起学习了枪法、剑术和空中飞人。”

“你在《热情如火》中从玛丽莲·梦露（Marilyn Monroe）那里学到了什么吗？”

他知道我在暗示什么，调皮地回答：“学会了萨克斯，但跟她没关系。”

看着我提着的黄色包包，托尼说：“你问了我这么多问题，现在轮到我问你一个了。为什么是这个黄色的包？它看起来像是和尚用的。”

“正是。”我告诉他，“我们在泰国拍戏的时候，我请了一位和尚，为我们祈祷天气放晴，他答应了。我们开始拍摄的那一刻，就开始下雨。这场雨持续了七天七夜。第八天，我去找那和尚‘抗议’。和尚回答说：‘孩子，下雨是为了农民，不是为了摄制组。’”

“那你跟和尚说了什么？”托尼问道。

“我只是鞠躬。我们成了好朋友。后来我发现他喜欢雪茄，就给他买了很多。他给了我这个和尚的包，我觉得它很轻巧。从此之后，我就一直背着它。”

“我喜欢你的故事。”托尼笑着给了我一个拥抱。

“我更喜欢你的。”

仇恨

佛经的教诲告诉我们不要杀生，但如果有我可以杀死的生物，我会杀死蚊子。我又恨又怕它们，它们的灭绝不会危害环境，我真的希望它们灭绝。

我出生在热带国家，从小就被蚊子困扰。小时候，我睡在蚊帐里，但总会有一两只“漏网之蚊”飞进来。我已经习惯了它们在我耳边嗡嗡作响，以至于我可以在睡觉的时候，把它们拍死。有时，当我醒来时，我会看到手臂或腿上有一个蜂巢状的红点。我知道我睡得离网太近了。

为了生存而吸我的血，是情有可原的，但为什么要让我有难以忍受的痒？

有一次我开车搭乘轮渡去马来西亚，在轮渡上，看到一片乌云向我袭来，声如雷鸣。

蚊子！

我马上冲回车里，并关起窗户。已经晚了！数以百计的蚊子跟着我进去。我的脸、胳膊和腿都被咬了。我差点痒死了。

真正的噩梦是我在泰国拍摄吴宇森导演的电影。

我们在丛林中建了一座房子，是在电影结束时拍摄爆炸场面用的。一切准备就绪。我们等到夜幕降临，便立即打开灯，这时，我们看到了一朵白色的“蚊子云”。在强光下，我们可以清晰地看到它们。它们的胃是透明的，它们渴望吸血！

它们每一只都属于“神风敢死队”。它们不惧怕死亡。它们飞向你，一旦咬住，就会粘在你的身上，不会飞走。

“保护演员！”我喊道，否则她们的脸会被咬得面目全非，不能继续拍摄。

整个晚上，我们一直在用风扇、苍蝇拍、杂志，以及任何我们可以用的东西杀死它们，但它们整晚一直进攻。

黎明破晓。蚊子小队又回到它们的阵地，我们也是。

噩梦还在继续，因为我们要连续拍七个晚上。

第二天晚上，我们带着驱虫剂、蚊香、电蚊拍和所有我们能找到的工具，全副武装地回来了。

“你脸上有一条红线！”女演员惊恐地尖叫起来。

我在镜子里也看到了。这条线就像一条路轨，从我的前额一直延伸到我的脸颊。一滴汗水洗掉了驱虫剂，蚊子找到了它们的梦想之地。

普通蚊子叮咬时，瘙痒会持续一个小时左右。这群不是。它们带来无穷无尽的难受。太痒了，你想用剃刀把被叮的位置切开。

夜漫长。只见当地摄制组一一消失。我发现他们睡眼迷蒙地躲在黑暗的角落里。有一股强烈的大麻味。这是暂时逃离的唯一方法。

又一个晚上过去了。

我们被动地迎战，我们都喝得大醉。

我喜欢一种叫作“湄公河”的当地威士忌。它装在扁平的小瓶子里，所以你可以把它放在你裤子的后口袋里。我一瓶接一瓶地喝，果然有效，没有那么多蚊子袭击我了。它们真的会享受，它们只攻击喝轩尼诗X.O.的香港工作人员。

另一个晚上。给我黄色袋子的和尚来拜访了。我问他怎么除蚊子。他回答说：“你靠拍电影谋生。这蚊子以吸血为生。摆脱它们，首先摆脱仇恨。这样也许会有所帮助。”

最后一晚，我做了一个梦。雷德利·斯科特（Ridley Scott）的电影中有一只和外星人一样大的蚊子。我知道害怕没用，所以我说：“你好！”

怪物点了点头。

“你现在一定厌倦了血液。来，试试这个。”我向怪物扔了一盒一加仑的冰淇淋。

它叮了一口，我肯定我看到它在微笑。

我给它一加仑又一加仑，直到它的胃撑破，数以百万计的小蚊子喷射而出！

我惊醒了。

奇怪的是，地上到处都是蚊子的尸体。

理发店

我在日本上学的时候就爱上了韩国。有一次假期，我从日本九州乘船到韩国釜山。

从那里，我乘火车前往首尔，在每个车站都停下来观光。

到了一个小镇，我觉得我需要理发了。在火车离开之前还有时间，我去了当地的一家理发店。先是一个老人给我剪了头发，然后是一个年轻人使劲地冲洗。接下来，一位年轻的女士走过来给我刮胡子。她首先在我的脸上抹了泡沫，然后用世界上最热的毛巾盖住我的脸！然后她用柔软的手指轻轻抚摸着我的胡须，再用锋利的剃须刀小心翼翼地将我的胡须一根一根地刮掉，同时有两个年轻人按摩着我的腿。最后，一位专家来挑掉我脸上的粉刺，然后另一位年轻女士再次回来给我刮脸。

噗噗噗！我听到火车鸣笛了！

我躺在理发椅上伸了个懒腰，告诉自己："我坐下一班车。"

伎生宴

我多次到韩国出差，与电影导演申相玉成了好朋友。他和我都在日本大学读书，所以我们有共同语言。

他到香港的时候，我请他吃各种美味的中国菜；我在韩国的时候，他给我安排了伎生宴。

伎生相当于韩国的“日本艺妓”。她们代表了一种娱乐贵宾的艺术。伎生宴的位置坐落在云雾缭绕的群山之中，宛如一幅古老的画卷。在冬天，她们烧松枝以制造适合神灵的香气。

宴席摆着一张长桌，放满了传统菜肴。每人三十碟菜，五个人共一百五十碟，如此类推。蜂蜜人参、红烧牛肉、迷你火锅、腌生蚝裹猪肉等等。

自己去拿食物是不可能的。你所要做的就是瞥一眼你最喜欢的菜，伎生会用一双银筷子把美食送到你的嘴里。

每位客人都与一名伎生配对。我看着她们，每一个都貌美如花，除了我身旁的那位，看起来很普通。我想知道为什么，我是客人，应该找最好的伎生来陪我。

我的伎生向我敬酒，我就喝了。她不屑地瞥了我一眼，把酒杯换成了大的玻璃杯。我们再干了一杯，但她的脸上依然充满不屑。[①]

最后，她把大碗里的汤倒掉，装满酒，一口气喝完。喝了十碗酒后，她站起来开始跳舞。伎生腰上绑着一个鼓，开始用两根棍子敲打。她不停地旋转，猛烈地击鼓。与此同时，服务员抬着一堵由

---

① 韩国人的习惯是一口气喝完一杯酒，再装满杯子，递给你喝完。然后你把杯子还给对方。一杯接一杯地来回传递，当你需要休息时，另一个伎生的杯子放在你的旁边，使它们成为一对。它们被称为“眼镜”，你会发现每个人都在嘲笑你。

十二个鼓组成的“鼓墙”进入大厅。然后突然一个动作，她向后弯下腰，将十二个鼓一个一个敲响。节奏越来越快，直到达到疯狂的高潮。一切都静止了。

她扑进了我的怀里。

唯一的动静就是她的胸膛上下起伏。

现在我知道为什么申相玉指定她来陪我了。

汉江船夫

韩国伎生从不和客人睡觉，但如果她欣赏你，那就是另一回事了。

我是个例外，我自认为是因为，我以温柔和尊重对待这位伎生。

韩国女性的社会地位比男性低，这是不可避免的，当时韩国的男女比例是一比七。韩国男人可以对他们的女人非常粗暴。你会听到像这样的老笑话：“我丈夫不爱我了，因为他最近没有打我。”

另一个笑话是，朝鲜战争前，男人比女人先走十步，女人在后面跟着。但战争结束后，女人比男人先走十步。当然，因为战后有地雷！

伎生和我一起度过了愉快的时光，晚饭后我们经常去汉江。岸边有许多船在等着。这些船长约三米，底部平坦。我们选了一艘，船夫把船划了出去。

他点燃了一支蜡烛，并用纸杯盖住了它。他对我的女朋友轻声说了几句，突然，他跳进河里游上了岸。

我们有了几个小时的独处时间，事后穿好衣服，伎生吹灭了蜡烛。

岸上的船夫看到信号，向我们游来。

这些都是美好的回忆，终生难忘。

寡妇

在我看来，韩国女性是亚洲最美丽的女性。

“但他们都做过整容手术呀！”我的朋友说。

胡说！我第一次到韩国时，朝鲜战争刚结束。她们衣衫褴褛，没钱吃饭，更别提整容手术了。你可能会问：“你怎样判断这些女人是最漂亮的？”你可以比较一下！

你去购物中心里的百货公司。在一个小时里，进行统计。

在首尔，你会遇到大约五位美女。

在台北三个。

在香港一个。

但在东京，如果你在银座待上三个小时，能遇见一个就算幸运了。

韩国女性大多个子很高，腰细，腿长，与亚洲其他地区的女性大不相同。

韩国女性的一大特点是坦率、大胆地表达自己的感受。爱的时候，是全心全意地爱；做爱的时候，是大声地呐喊。在那个年代，韩国酒店房间的墙壁很薄。你可以听到女人大喊：“Yobo！Yobo！”这意思是，“亲爱的！亲爱的！”，有时挺尴尬的。

当我制作一部需要雪景的功夫片时，我的好朋友申相玉把他的摄制组借给了我。这是一个与申相玉密切合作多年的摄制组。拍摄地点没有路，我们不得不徒步攀登雪山。我曾在许多国家工作过，但我从未遇到过像那些韩国人那样努力工作的摄制组。男人背着沉重的装备，女人也背着沉重的装备。

摄制组里有一位服装设计师对我很好。当我们休息时，她总是设法给我热茶。韩国人喜欢咖啡，很少喝茶，所以我不知道她是怎么在深山里找到茶叶和热水的。她三十多岁了，从不抱怨辛苦，脸上总挂着微笑。我从摄影师那里听说她是寡妇。她的丈夫曾是申相玉的副导演。许多年后，申认为是时候让她的丈夫执导一部自己的电影了。有了机会，他努力工作，但因为电影票房失败，他自杀了。寡妇没有再婚，继续为申相玉工作。

剧组成员之间经常发生恋情，但作为剧组的领导，我会远离这种事情。我有一个座右铭——不要在你吃饭的地方拉屎！尽管如此，寡妇和我之间的联系每天都在加强。

当我们在一条小溪附近拍摄最后一个场景时，我听到特技师大喊“合成血浆”。没有人能找到它，然后我想起它被留在了小溪的另一边。为了不浪费时间，我趟过小溪，把血浆带到特技师那里。回来时，因为冰冷的水，我的脚没有任何感觉。

寡妇想都没想，打开毛衣，把我冻僵的脚塞在裸露的胸前。

我深受触动。

拍完之后我们就没有再见面，但每年都会交换贺年卡。

多年后，我突然接到了她的电话。

“我在香港。”

“你好吗？”我忍不住问，“你还在为申先生工作吗？”

“我辞职了。我开了一家小时装店，我是来买东西的。”她回答道。我放下电话，赶往她的旅馆。

她开了门。现在我们不再是同事了，我们没有什么可担心的。我检查了墙壁，它们很厚。

没有人能听到我们的声音。

倪匡趣事

倪匡是我最好的朋友之一。他是香港电影界最多产的编剧。李小龙的所有电影的剧本都是他写的。他还是中国最好的科幻小说家，著有畅销书五百本。

我从不厌倦讲述他生活中有趣的故事，这是其中一部分……

倪匡和酒

倪匡年轻时酗酒，后来成了酒鬼。他每天至少喝两瓶750毫升的白兰地和1.5升的伏特加。

三个神父来到他家，告诉他酒精的危害有多大。

“你一定知道耶稣创造的第一个奇迹吧？”他回答说，“上帝从来没有告诉过你不要喝酒。他只是说你必须高兴地喝酒。”

但有一天，突然间，他确实戒了酒。当他的朋友问他为什么时，他回答说：“上帝告诉我的！”

“请详细告诉我们。”我们都说。

“我讨厌被酒精控制，并多次尝试戒酒。人们告诉我，戒酒比戒毒更难。有一天，我遇到一位神父，我问他：‘如果两个人一起祈祷，上帝会垂听我们，是真的吗？’

“‘是的，’牧师回答说，‘圣经是这么说的。’

“‘那就和我一起祈祷吧。’我请求道。

“于是我们一起祷告。

“从第二天开始，我一滴酒也没碰过！”

我们都认为上帝确实行了神迹。

“我们的生活是有配额的，”倪后来说，“也许我的酒都喝光了。”

他的朋友说："但我们看到你和蔡澜喝酒了！"

"他是美酒鉴赏家！他只买最好的。我的坏酒配额可能已经用完了，但好酒的配额才刚刚开始！"

倪匡和收音机

倪匡在生活中兴趣广泛，他努力学习，成为所有这些方面的专家。

有一段时间他收集贝壳。他收集了这么多，以至于他不得不租一套公寓来展示它们！他关于贝壳的论文得到了国际贝壳学学术界的认可！

他还是热带鱼方面的专家。

他养殖了数千条。他从亚马逊购买浓缩水，然后在鱼缸中稀释，以安抚鱼儿的思乡之情。

他订造了许多鱼缸，是六英尺[①]长的巨大长方体，当倪太太埋怨的时候，他就说："它们是完美的棺材！"

在他生命中的另一个时期，对制作家具感兴趣，他做了一个又一个橱柜。不确定成品是否完美，他会把儿子锁在里面问："你能看到任何光吗？"

当然，他的儿子大喊："不！不！"

我们钦佩他掌握这些不同事物的技能。有一天我去探望他的时候，发现他办公桌上有六七台收音机。

---

① 1英尺约0.3米。——编者注

他注意到了我的好奇心。“我喜欢在写作时听音乐。”他解释道。

“是的，但为什么这么多？”

“哦，”他耸了耸肩，“我不会调频道！”

加藤和尚

每次经过寺院，我都会想起他。

加藤是我在日本留学时最好的朋友之一。

我们在新宿经常光顾的咖啡馆叫风月堂，那里聚集了许多艺术家。一天晚上，一个美国嬉皮士给了他半支大麻烟。当他离开时，他被警察逮捕，但随后被保释。

庭审前，他号召他所有的朋友捐钱给他聘请一位好律师。不是为他辩护，而是让他可以提出大麻不像酒精那样有害的主张。他已经准备好进监狱。现在医用大麻已在许多国家合法化，这个故事似乎具有讽刺意味。

我离开日本后，我的前任秘书曾写信给我说加藤出家了，有一天他会来香港看我。在一次访问日本时，我发现他不再住在那里，而是在世界各地流浪。

多年后，他穿着黄色的长袍出现在嘉禾工作室。我很高兴再次见到他。

“走吧，我们去吃素菜吧。”我说。

“不，如果你不介意的话，我宁愿你带我回家，给我煮些饺子。我非常想念它们。”

在学生时代，我们很穷，几个月都没有肉吃。等我有钱了，就买些便宜的碎猪肉给朋友包饺子。

“饺子里有肉。”我提醒他。

“没关系。我没吃肉。我吃的是回忆。”他回答道。

饭后，我带他参观了香港，并带他参加了我的新电影的首映礼。

有很多娱乐媒体的记者。每个人都很想知道一个和尚到底在做什么。加藤喜欢和女演员们合影，并且非常习惯相机的闪光。

“这在佛教中被称为幻影。”他笑着说。

第二天，他跟我道别。

“从现在开始你要做什么？”我问。

“我要回到马萨诸塞州的一座寺庙。我会试着在那里建一座宝塔。”

我再也没有见过加藤，但每年新年我都会收到他的善意经。

他确实在马萨诸塞州建造了一座宏伟的宝塔。

另一个和尚：牛次郎

我还有一个日本朋友也是和尚。

牛次郎的意思是“牛的次子”，这是他的笔名。我不记得他的真名是什么。除了在日本的一个小岛经营寺庙外，他还为日本漫画写过故事，它们都是畅销书。

我想把他写的故事拍成电影，所以我安排在我住的银座帝国酒店跟他见面。他开着他的古董梅赛德斯-奔驰。

“这家酒店的天妇罗餐厅相当不错。我们去吃。”他说。

“和尚不是应该吃素的吗？”我问。

“好东西例外。”他开玩笑地说，“他们也可以结婚。”

牛次郎很瘦，戴着一副圆框眼镜。他的头发被剪短了，他的牙齿被烟熏黑了。

“你真的是和尚吗？”我直接问了。

“日本僧人代代相传。我出生在和尚家庭。”

“谢谢你来东京看我。”我说。

“没什么，我这里有办公室。”

“办公室？”

“这不是真正的办公室，更像是我写作的书房。我也方便见见我的女朋友们。”他笑着说。

那天晚上我们边吃边聊，直到餐厅关门。我们有很多共同的兴趣。

“哪天到我的庙里来看看。”他向我道别。

我答应了。

过了一段时间，我从热海乘船到达了他的岛。

牛次郎的寺庙位于山顶，比我想象的要大得多。面朝大海，风景很美。

寺庙后面是他的住所。他带我直奔他的酒柜，那里有无数瓶陈年美酒。我们开始尽情地喝酒。

“经营寺庙是一项垂死的事业，”他说，“这就是我必须写作的原因。”

“无论你做什么，你都非常成功。”

“对我的生活方式来说还不够。”

“我听说人们在为死者举行葬礼上花了很多钱。”

牛次郎叹了口气，“没有了。他们宁愿把钱花在生活上。此外，日本人的寿命越来越长。建一座寺庙可赚的钱很少”。

我不知道怎么安慰他。

“但是，”他高兴起来，“我发明了一项新业务！”

他把我带到他花园的后面。在那里我看到了一个非常大的焚化炉。他像拍他的新玩具一样拍拍它。

“这是用来烧猫狗尸体的。”

“所以？”

牛次郎雄辩道：“如你所知，拥有温泉的热海是退休夫妇的理想去处。他们的儿子和女儿很少去看望他们。所以他们养宠物作伴，并变得非常依恋它们。动物的寿命较短，当它们死去时，它们的主人想为它们做一切可能的事情。就在这时，我想到了焚化炉！死去的动物可以在这里火化。费用为20万日元。如果主人要我超度，另外还要20万日元。如果你把它们埋在寺庙里，并立一个墓碑，那就是100万日元。它已成为一项非常有利可图的服务，人们必须排队等候。老人们花钱的时候，比他们的儿女花在他们身上的还要慷慨！”

我完全明白了。不过有一件事仍然让我感到困惑。

“猫和狗很小。为什么要建这么大的焚化炉？”

他眼中闪过一丝光彩，回答道：“有时我的妻子太啰嗦了。”

在玩乐中体验人生

把头靠在我肩上

上中学的时候，我是一群顽童里的一员，我们总是逃课跑出来看电影。

其中一个男孩来自马来西亚的一个小镇。他的亲戚在新加坡买了房子，让他打理。在假期里，我们这帮人会在家里举办派对，并邀请我们认识的女孩们彻夜跳舞。

其中有一位留着长发的少女，我们还在读书的时候，她已经在工作了。在那个年纪，我们都喜欢更成熟的女孩，我们一直和她一起跳舞。

音乐从摇滚乐变成了慢节奏的歌曲。保罗·安卡（Paul Anka）的《把头靠在我肩上》是最受欢迎的歌曲。我们拥抱在一起。

后来我的朋友娶了这个美丽的长发女人。我是伴郎和司机。我们开车去了他的小镇。有一辆货车在等，里面坐着当地乐队。他们演奏了《桂河大桥》的主题曲来欢迎我们。顺便说一句，他们在葬礼上也玩过同样的事情！

当地的传统是新娘和新郎在镇上转三圈宣布他们结婚了，我们也这样做了。

婚礼在学校礼堂举行。每个人都被邀请了。校长被要求发表演讲。他不是每天都有这样的机会，所以他演讲了一个小时，每个人都睡着了。我在晚宴上喝醉了。第二天早上，我们分开了。

直到十年后，我们才再次相见。我从国外回来看我的朋友。他现在在高速公路上经营一个加油站。他告诉我，他们结婚后，他的妻子开了一家美容院。生意很好。毕竟她来自大城市，知道所有最新的发型。但悲剧发生了。她得了小儿麻痹症，腰部以下都瘫痪了。

“赶快！带我去见她！”我感到窒息。

他们住在一间灯光昏暗的中国老房子里。看到她头发凌乱，脸色苍白，心里很难受。我们三个紧紧地抱在一起哭了起来。冷静下来，她问道：“你还记得我们是怎么把橙汁、柠檬汁和一整瓶杜松子酒混合在一起的吗？”

“你还记得你害羞到我拉你起来和我跳舞吗？”

“你还记得我们喝醉之后，赤身裸体挤在一条大毯子下吗？”

“是的是的。”我忍住了眼泪。

月亮照在椰子树的顶端。我的朋友把她背在背上。我们三个人走在村子里的一条小路上。我们去那里看“波莫”，相当于马来语中的巫师。她听说他可以创造奇迹，坚持要试一试。我答应了。

我们走进一间竹屋。地上坐着几十个人。他们都带来了水果、银器、衣服、鸡和鸡蛋等礼物。波莫没有说谢谢，就接受了。

一名助手点燃了一些香料木。房间里充满了烟雾。这让气氛更加诡异。

波莫开始施展他的魔法。

他的手一挥，就发生了小小的爆炸。当他拉回地板上的垫子时，绿色宝石和红宝石出现了。所有人都惊呆了。

所有前来求救的人都聚拢得更近。波莫摸了一个生病的孩子的头。他立即被治愈了。一个男人肿胀的肚子变平了。

轮到我们了。波莫拿出一个鸡蛋，在女孩的腿上蹭了蹭。然后他在碗里打碎了鸡蛋。小红虫从鸡蛋里溢出，在碗里膨胀扭动。它们还活着！

我的朋友和他的妻子深深鞠躬并提供礼物。

我在拍电影时就知道这些技巧。

波莫周围的人显然是他的同党。那些小虫子是被压缩的红纸，藏在他的手指里。当纸张接触到液体，它膨胀得像蠕虫一样蠕动。

我不忍心告诉他们真相。我怎么忍心？

他们很高兴。他们在回家的路上一直唱着《把头靠在我肩上》。

我再也没有见过他们。

一抹色彩

丁雄泉（Walasse Ting）的画总是让我充满快乐。充满活力的色彩和欢乐的画面，如何能不喜欢呢？如果我能学到他的一点，我就很高兴了。

我很想认识他，有一天他在香港举办他的展览时，一位报界的朋友把我们介绍给了彼此。丁雄泉身材高大魁梧。虽然他已经六十多岁了，但看上去比较年轻。丁先生因为我对他的作品了解而感到惊喜，并说他喜欢阅读我的文章，我们可以成为朋友。我拒绝了。我恳求成为他的学生。

“我永远不会教你画画，”他说，“因为我从来没有学过画画。”

“真的吗？”我问。

“看看我的作品。所有的线条都像孩子的涂鸦。正是这些颜色吸引了人们。”

“那就教我怎么用颜色吧。”

“成为著名画家是你的志向吗？如果是这样，你就太迟了。需要一生的时间才有机会成为一个普通的艺术家，更不用说成为一个好艺术家了。在你这个年纪，你只能领略到一点。”

“这就是我想要的。”

“好吧，那我们就成为朋友吧。”

“那就做朋友吧。”我最后说。

从那以后，他去中国或远东其他地区旅行时，我抓住一切机会与他见面。

有一次在上海，我们去了一家著名的餐厅。丁先生点了菜单上几乎所有的菜。“我在阿姆斯特丹不是每天都能吃到美味的中国菜。”他说。

服务员走过来，看到一桌菜：“只有你们两个？你邀请了谁却没来？”

“哦，”丁先生说，“我们邀请了李白、毕加索、爱因斯坦等等。”

我特意去阿姆斯特丹，因为丁先生就住在那里。我一大早就到了。

杰西，丁先生的儿子在机场接我。从那以后，我也成了他们整个家庭的朋友。丁先生有一个儿子和一个住在纽约的女儿米娅。

我在希尔顿酒店订了房间，列侬（Lennon）和洋子（Yoko）拍了那些著名的照片的同一个房间。

丁先生的房子曾经是一所古老的中学。木门很小，他在上面画满了野花。杰西说门被偷了两次。当我进入时，我看到了任何艺术家都梦寐以求的巨大工作室。这是一个改建的室内篮球馆。天花板有三层楼高，内衬着五百管荧光灯，这样丁先生就可以将阴天变成暑假。

一股强烈的洋葱香味扑鼻而来。它来自数百个孤挺花球茎。它们似乎在同一时间盛开。

“我们喝酒！”丁先生拿出了一个陈年水晶瓶。

“我们早上应该喝香槟吗？”我问。

“我们应该晚上才喝香槟吗？”他回答。

喝完第一瓶后，他打开了第二瓶。

“那么，”我说，“我如何开始像你一样使用绚丽的色彩？”

“别学我，向自然学习。任何五颜六色的东西都是你的老师。看看刚刚飞进花园的翠鸟。仔细看。你能看到它羽毛的颜色吗？记住它，研究它，重新创造它。”

“我应该用什么颜料？”

“我发现丙烯更光亮。最好的是名为Flashe的法国产品。你可以像溶解水彩一样溶解它，也可以像画油画一样使用它。”

他描绘了一个黑白色的女人身影，说：“去吧，涂上颜色。”

回想起他的许多画作，我在上面泼洒了一些颜色。他点了点头。几瓶香槟被喝光了。课堂一直持续到午夜。那个时候我喝醉了，倒在他的沙发上睡着了。

第二天，我们去了艾伯特市场，买了很多的食物。最令人愉快的是我们像当地人一样吃生鲱鱼，抬起头整条放进嘴里，然后大口咀嚼。我们回到工作室做饭、画画和喝酒。那是我一生中最值得怀念的时刻。

"我应该在什么地方作画？"我问。

"任何东西上，"他回答，"纸、布、冰箱。任何单调乏味的东西。给它们上色。使它们栩栩如生。给它们和自己带来快乐。"

我做到了，我甚至给我的手提箱刷了漆。当我通过海关时，人们会认出它们。"丁雄泉？"他们笑着问。

后来我买了一千条白色的领带，也画了。我不介意人们称我为模仿者。如果我能从丁雄泉身上继承一丝色彩，我的余生都会幸福。

杰西的狗

丁雄泉有一位美籍犹太裔妻子。她离世后，他们十几岁的儿子丁杰西悲痛欲绝，失去了活下去的意志。

丁先生觉得去泰国苏梅岛旅行会减轻他的痛苦，但杰西到了之后，一直呆坐，看着游泳池。

一天，杰西听到一声奇怪的呻吟，便去寻找来源。他发现了一条最丑的狗，一条真正的杂种狗。它的身体上布满了伤口，瘦得连骨头都看得见。杰西很同情它，把早餐剩下的面包扔给了狗。那条狗一口气把它吞了下去。杰西扔了一个西红柿，狗也吃了。事实上，它太饿了，什么都吃。

从那以后，这条狗时刻跟着杰西。

整个苏梅岛到处都是椰子树和森林。这只狗只是默默地走到杰西身后。

当他口渴时，他注意到狗会舔树叶上的晨露。它一直在寻找吃的东西。有时它会翻石头吃蚂蚁，就像一只穿山甲。杰西发现这只狗有如此强烈的求生意志，这让他感到羞耻。

有一天，这只狗失踪了，杰西到处寻找它。

酒店的服务员问道："少爷，您找什么？"

"你在附近有没有见到狗？"

"岛上到处都是流浪狗。我们用网捕捉它们。我听同事说，我们刚刚抓到了一只。"

"那条狗现在在哪里？"杰西焦急地问道。

"通常它们会被带到警察局被M16枪杀。"

"都是我的错，"杰西想，"如果我没有喂狗，它就不会被抓住。"

冲出酒店的杰西乘坐出租车前往警察局。

"嗒嗒嗒嗒！"听到一连串枪响。太迟了！太迟了！杰西一生中从未感到如此内疚。他在血泊中发现了许多狗，但没有一条狗比他所爱的狗更丑。

他回到酒店，正在游泳池旁呆坐着，那只狗又出现在了他的身边。杰西立刻抱住了它。

酒店工作人员后来告诉杰西，有人看到这只狗从警车里逃了出来。

从此，杰西和他的狗形影不离。

“爸爸，我可以留着它吗？”丁先生看到了儿子和狗乞求的眼神。他终于点了点头。

将动物从泰国带到荷兰是一项艰巨的任务。首先，你必须给它买一张比乘客还贵的机票。然后，你必须从兽医那里获得健康证明，并在此之前行贿。对于杰西的狗，必须制作一个特殊的笼子，因为当地航空公司从未有过这种经历。

贿赂海关官员又是必需的。丁先生和他的儿子回到兽医那里，因为根据泰国法律，必须给他一剂强力镇静剂。

兽医说：“你必须知道，狗可能会有危险。”决定下了，狗似乎也接受了。当兽医打针时，狗没有反抗。

他们的麻烦似乎无穷无尽。没有直飞阿姆斯特丹的航班，他们不得不在法兰克福转机。

当他们降落在那里时，航空公司的工作人员找不到那只狗。

“也许它已经在高空中冻死了。”他们说。

经过长时间的搜索，他们发现这只狗已经打破了笼子，跑到了餐饮区，它在那里大口吃着头等舱的饭菜，现在正在安静地睡觉。

此时杰西拒绝再让那条狗从他身边离开。他们在法兰克福下机，雇了一辆车直接开回阿姆斯特丹。

杰西搬到了一座四面高墙的乡间别墅，防止狗跑丢。他悉心照料着这只狗，让它恢复健康，到了冬天，它长出了一层可爱的长毛。事实上，这只狗吃得太好了，不得不让它节食！

这是一只恶霸！多年来，杰西的狗杀死了附近家庭的无数鸡鸭，以及两只小山羊。

时不时，那条狗会面向遥远故乡所在的东方，嚎叫，嚎叫，嚎叫。

我的书法同学

丁雄泉的人生充满了绚丽的色彩，而冯康侯大师的世界却黑白分明。

在我四十岁那年，我感到我的生命正在消逝，我知道我必须做些事情。

最简单的解决方法是将艺术作为一种爱好。当我还是个孩子的时候，我父亲会用毛笔写各种各样的书法来哄我。我一直想像他一样，但我的电影工作实在太忙，我差不多把所有事情都忘记了。但是我父亲种下了一颗种子，是时候让它开花了。

于是我去找了香港最好的书法家冯先生，请他教我。

在我上第一堂课的那天，他最爱的儿子死于肺炎。我在考虑是否应该找另一天再来，但我决定敲门。

“进来，进来，”他说，“哀悼是没有用的。我宁愿坚强下来教你。”

他拿出一张纸，让我写点什么，随便什么。

“但我不知道如何开始。”我抗议道。

“想到什么就写什么。”

我终于写下：“感谢您收我为徒。”

“从你的文字中，我知道哪位大师的风格最接近你的风格。这位大师留下了许多手稿。你可以向他学习。我小时候也跟他学过。当我们都向同一位老师学习时，我们就是同学。”

我含着眼泪握住了他的手。

从此，我日日夜夜疯狂地练书法。

微笑的小红

小红总是微笑着。如果她不是那么漂亮，人们会说她很单纯。她被称为小红，因为她光滑的皮肤和红润的脸颊。

像许多古老的故事一样，她的母亲生了九个孩子，大女儿小红不得不工作，养家糊口。十七岁的时候，当被问到“你想做什么”，她举起手说：“我要喝酒跳舞。”她做到了。

“新加坡舞厅”是七十年代台北最好的歌舞表演地。那里的经理立即看到了小红的潜力。小红不仅是一位出色的舞者，她还能像鱼一样喝酒。纯的白兰地一杯接一杯地喝，反正她的脸颊本来就是红润的！令所有人惊讶的是，她从来没有喝醉过。

“喝酒！”客户要求。

倒了一大杯白兰地，小红从来没有拒绝过。一饮而尽，顾客会躺在桌子底下，而小红只是保持微笑。这使她成为歌舞表演中最赚钱的资产，她的名声传得很快。镇上所有的有钱人都挤进了舞厅，为了看她一眼。每个人都发誓他可以让小红喝醉，但没有人成功。

她的追求者中有两位每天晚上都来。一位是著名艺术家的儿子，另一位是富商的儿子。前者又瘦又高，神情忧郁。小红注意到他的手指像钢琴家的一样修长。后者很胖，吃得跟猪一样。他总是和商业伙伴一起来，让他们结账。好吧，你可以猜到小红喜欢哪一位。

一天晚上，悲剧发生了。两人之间爆发了一场争吵，但经理能够处理它并制止了斗殴。然而，当艺术家的儿子从歌舞厅出来时，他被商人的儿子和他的帮派伏击，他们用武士刀袭击了他，艺术家的儿子试图自卫，结果三根手指被砍下来了。警察来到的时候，那伙人已经逃跑了。艺术家的儿子被紧急送往医院。手指被重新缝合，但他没有机会演奏钢琴了。

小红辞掉了工作，嫁给了他。他们搬到东京居住，丈夫在那里为一家大公司工作。他们生了两个孩子，孩子们很快就长大了。

丈夫回家的次数越来越少，但小红从不抱怨。

有一天，小红宣布："我要当一名妈妈桑。"

"你得为我的名誉考虑一下！"丈夫对她大喊大叫。

小红没有争辩，她笑了笑，还是我行我素。

她工作的酒吧在银座。只有富商才能负担得起这里的消费。小红虽然已经三十四岁，可她的腰围还是二十四岁，喝起酒来还像条鱼。丈夫最终接受了现实。"反正妈妈桑也不跟顾客睡觉。"他心里想。

一天晚上，一位台湾男子走进来。酒吧女郎告诉他，她们有一个从未喝醉过的妈妈桑。他很好奇地呼唤她。

"喝了。"他命令到。

女孩们惊讶地看到妈妈桑只喝了一杯酒就醉了，更惊讶的是她同意去他的旅馆。

在酒店房间里，他们喝了一杯又一杯，直到商人倒下并变得无意识。 小红放下瓶子，把男人拉起来，把他的右臂放在两把椅子之间。她爬上椅子，然后往他的手臂跳下去。那人大声哭了起来，但他喝醉了，动弹不得。她把他的手臂以不同的角度再做一次，以确保骨头完全破碎。

然后她笑着离开。

你可以猜到那个人是谁。

古堡女伯爵

七十年代我们在巴塞罗那度过了非常美好的时光！伊比利亚火腿、西班牙银鱼和鬼爪螺，在当时的美食界都鲜为人知，而且价格合理。参观完博物馆后，我们在波盖利亚市场数公斤数公斤地买这些美食。我们在“圣家堂”（圣家族教堂的简称）旁边租了公寓，这样我们可以在有空的时候研究高迪（Gaudi）的作品。

言归正传。我们在那里拍摄《快餐车》，电影中需要为最后一幕建造一座大城堡。在探索了许多地点后，我们选好了一个，但城堡的主人伯爵夫人拒绝将其借给我们。

经过无休止的谈判，伯爵夫人终于同意见我。

“她是什么样的人？”我问我们的西班牙外景经理。

“她看起来就是一只吸血鬼。当你看到她时，你就会明白我的意思。”他回答道。

那天晚上，我被邀请到城堡和她共进晚餐。我满怀期待地来到大门口。他们自动打开门，对讲机上发出阴森森的命令声音：“走到走廊尽头！”

前往餐厅的路似乎没有终点，我想象着我的脖子被钉出两个洞，鲜血喷涌而出。我打开沉重的门，看到一位瘦弱的老太太，她看起来和外景经理描述的一模一样。她伸出她那只瘦骨嶙峋的手，我像个绅士一样亲吻了它。她笑了。在我的脑海中，我可以看到尖牙！

桌上已经摆好了冷盘。

“你一定想知道为什么城堡是空的，”她说，“优雅的时代已经结束，现在的我，尽量远离人群。”

开了一瓶红酒。

“噢！”我哭着说，“塞拉丽亚酒庄的特索修道院罗马尼克！”

“喝吧，”她说，“我的地窖里有数百瓶酒，但已经没多少光阴让我把库存喝光。”

我感觉到一种悲伤的语气，然后说：“我们总有一天要走的。重要的是我们过着充实的生活。”她点点头。晚饭后，她拿出了一本相册。我看到她年轻的时候参加温布尔登网球公开赛、在金字塔前摆姿势、参观中国长城和威尼斯运河。

酒很甜，我们听着彼此的故事，开怀大笑。

“当我们认识彼此时，我们看起来并不那么可怕，你同意吗？”

我点点头，向她告别。获得了拍摄许可。

一天早上，我们拍摄的时候，在城堡里遇到了一位身着网球服的美丽少女。我可以发誓我以前在什么地方见过她。她走过来对我说：“我是来陪你的。奶奶告诉我，你是一个有趣的人。”

吐金鱼的人

我在游乐场长大。

我父亲是经理，我们住在游乐场后面。20世纪50年代，游乐园是一个巨大的开放空间，有电影院、歌舞表演、歌剧舞台和许多商店。只有在晚上挤满了人的时候，它才会活跃起来。白天，它相当冷清。

我喜欢放学后四处闲逛，看胖摔跤手做骗人的动作，魔术师练习纸牌技巧，功夫学徒互相打架。我也很喜欢福建剧团的表演，还和小京剧演员交上了朋友。

有一个露天舞台，让流浪艺人大显身手。

一天，一位老人带着他十几岁的女儿来了。我清楚地记得，他的左脸颊上有纵横交错的伤疤，手指也变形了。

他喝了一杯水，然后用嘴唇形成一个狭窄的洞，将一股水流吹回玻璃杯中。一、二、三，他重复这个动作，把水倒回三个杯子里。我们被迷住了。接着，他拿起一个大鱼缸，把整缸水喝光了，包括里面的金鱼。我们屏住呼吸，等着看接下来会发生什么。老人喉咙里发出一声低吼，顿时把水全部倒了回去，金鱼还在游动。我们都鼓起掌来。

父女俩在公园里安顿下来，每天晚上表演。每次表演完后，女儿都会从观众那里收钱。她的脸颊红润，皮肤白得像雪一样。在热带国家，这是我们很少看到的。

随着时间的推移，越来越少的人来看他的表演。

老人还有一些绝招。他的另一个绝技是用跳蚤表演的。他的跳蚤可以按照他的命令从一只手臂跳到另一只手臂上。他还为跳蚤制作了精细的迷你卡车、坦克和带轮子的银色大炮。它们可以拉动一百倍于自身重量的东西。表演结束后，老人向观众展示了他的手臂以及跳蚤是如何吸他的血的。他说："我养跳蚤，跳蚤养我。"所有人都欢呼起来。

我从我父亲的同事那里听说，老人和他的妻子曾经是上海最著名的空中飞人。在一次意外中他摔下来了，伤了他的脸和手，失去了他的妻子。从此，他不得不四处游荡，强迫自己做其他事情。

我和老人的女儿Shia Shia成了好朋友。她常到我们家借书。我爸爸是个知识分子，他收藏了一屋子的书。Shia Shia总是唱英文歌，她最喜欢的一首是《在我们小时候》。我记得一个炎热的下午，听着她的歌声，我的眼皮变得沉重，我在她的怀里睡着了。他们的宿舍没有合适的浴室，所以有时Shia Shia会过来问，她是否可以使用我们的浴室。有一次，我不小心从门缝里看到了她丰满的乳房。我尴尬到脸都红了。我羞愧得在游乐园里跑了三圈。

人们厌倦了跳蚤表演。老人不得不掏出最后绝招。

台上放着一个长方形的木箱，老爷子拿出十六把利剑，吩咐女儿穿一件比基尼，进入木箱。然后，他将剑一把一把推进了盒子里。每推一把剑，观众都大声喊叫，他们又害怕又期待。十六把剑全部插好后，老人说观众可以花一分钱看看这把戏是怎么做的。当然，我是第一个冲上去看看发生了什么的人。在那里，我看到Shia Shia扭着身子，一寸一寸地避开剑。一分钱，一分钱，你可以看到Shia Shia的身体！

“不！不！”我哭了。

我从Shia Shia的眼里看到她也在哭。她知道我受到了深深的伤害，但她很无助。我觉得很丢脸，远远跑开，眼泪从我的眼睛里流出来。之后几天我都对他们避而不见，然后我发烧生病了。等我痊愈的时候，他们已经不见了。显然，观众并不觉得这个行为有趣。我再也没有见过Shia Shia。

多年后，当我住在日本时，我走在街上，听到有人在叫我的小名。

我转过身，看到了老人。我激动得说不出话来。我把他拉到一家高档餐厅，点了我能想到的所有食物。

“Shia Shia怎么样？”我急切地问道。

“她离开了我，跟马戏团的人跑了。”他回答道。

我不知道怎么安慰他。

看着盘子，他说：“我好饿。”

“吃吧。”我说。

“我不能。”

“不能？什么意思？”

“我是实验室里的一只老鼠。”

“你说你是一只老鼠，是什么意思？实验室？”

我们离开的时候，老人解释道：“一个制药公司的教授看到了我吞咽金鱼的表演。他雇我做食物消化的实验。每天早上我必须吞下两个鸡蛋，根据他们需要收集的数据，我得在指定时间内把它们吐出来。我只知道我的胃必须整天都是空的。这就是为什么我这么饿。”

“去他妈的日本人！”我大喊。

“日本人养我，我必须养日本人。”老人喃喃自语，消失在人群中。

鱼贩

旺角露天市场笼罩在晨雾中。在清晨的薄雾里，这是一幅黑白摄影杰作的理想图像。

小贩中有一个年轻的鱼贩。那是一个夏日。他上身赤裸，露出全身的肌肉。

在他面前有一个大竹篮，里面装满了鳗鱼，每一条都有长黄瓜那么大，都是活的，活蹦乱跳的。

中国人视鳗鱼为美味佳肴，据说吃鳗鱼可以提高性能力。

他一把抓住一条，把它的头钉在砧板上。然后用锋利的刀熟练地切下了皮和骨头。客人把鳗鱼买回去就可以煮。我从他那里买了几公斤并先付了钱。

“你是个好人，”他评论道，“顾客通常在我准备好鳗鱼后才付款。”

“都一样。”我说。

“不。如果你先付钱，警察来的时候我可能会跑掉，然后你就亏了。”

“所以你是无牌小贩？”

“这里没有人有牌照。”他笑着说。

“警察每天都来吗？”

“每天，9点整，准时。我们都准备在他们来之前离开，他们走后才回来。”

我笑道：“这很英式。在马来战争中，他们的空军逢周一、周三和周五投下炸弹。敌军只在周二、周四和周六才出来。”

鱼贩问：“那周日呢？”

“周日，双方都休息了。”我们一起笑了起来。

就在这个时候，一个女人出现了。

“我可以选一些鳗鱼吗？”

“当然可以。”年轻人回答。这名女子三十多岁，身穿紧身中式连衣裙，露出她女性的身体。她一条一条地挑着鳗鱼，抚摸着它们，她的呼吸变得沉重起来。阳光照在青年身后，勾勒出他肌肉和汗水的轮廓。

年轻人一句话也没说就走了，丢下所有的东西，把所有的鳗鱼都给了邻近的鱼贩。那一刻，我还以为警察提早来了。

然后我看到那对青年男女消失在人群中。

永恒的骗局

多年前，我遇到了一个侦探，他跟我讲了莹莹的故事。

老张是香港上海银行的初级职员。他的工作单调乏味，生活乏味。一天晚上，老张路过庙街，这是一个肮脏的地方，在书报摊上看到了一本杂志封面，上面有一张日本艳星的裸照。她没有化妆，长着一张天使的脸。老张一下子就爱上了她。他突然有了一个主意。

第二天，他用相机把杂志封面拍出三张照片。第一张是艳星的脸，第二张是上半身，最后一张是全身。在那之后，他请一个朋友把每张照片冲印了两千份。

最后，他在不同的邮局租用了许多信箱。照片和信箱都不便宜，但老张愿意投资。随后，他辞掉了工作，在家中努力干活。

他从美国、英国、加拿大和澳大利亚购买杂志，并从笔友专栏中记下潜在客户。然后他把信寄给他们，每封信件里面，都有一张艳星的头像。

亲爱的约翰、唐纳德、安东尼，名字不同，但内容相同：

“我叫莹莹，今年十八岁。我家里有八个兄弟姐妹。我们的父母年老体弱。作为老大，我必须在酒吧做服务员。顾客觉得我很漂亮，每天晚上都来。他们提出要带我出去。作为传统中国人，我的道德价值观，让我拒绝了他们，保持自己的贞洁。”

老张用钢笔把每封信都写得很整齐。

生活对他来说变得有趣了。有些信件得到了同情的回信。

老张继续写回信：“我最大的愿望是去美国深造。可惜，我甚至不得不用我存下来的30美元签证申请费，来为我最小的妹妹支付医疗费。”

当时30港元大约是2美元。每个人都愿意提供帮助。老张充满诚意地向他们表示感谢。之后的一些回信，会询问莹莹是否收到付款以及她的签证申请进度如何。

“你想要更多的钱去申请其他国家的签证吗？”

莹莹道：“我怎么能强加给你？你做的已经够多了。”

下一封信来了，里面有更多的钱。在这些信件中，最热情的一封来自俄克拉何马州的一位律师。让我们称他为吉米。

“我亲爱的吉米，”莹莹写道，“你是我的救星！我日日夜夜想你。我整个人都兴奋起来。不知不觉我的内裤湿了。对一个年轻女孩来说，写信告诉你这件事真是太可耻了。”

当然，同一封信也寄给了乔、亚当、路易斯、约瑟夫等等。“附言：你能给我发一张你的照片让我看看你的肌肉吗？”莹莹写道。

更多的钱寄给了她，包括要求的照片，他们也问了莹莹同样的问题。

“最亲爱的约翰，我做了我一生中最大胆的事情。我请我的闺蜜为我拍了这张照片。这是为了报答你的恩情。你会认为我很低俗吗？我很担心。”

一张张露出粉红色乳头的半裸照片寄出去了。大量的回信和美元回邮，填满了邮箱。单是俄克拉何马州的律师吉米，就寄了几百封信，但最慷慨的是来自沙特阿拉伯的那个人，他寄了几千封。吉米写道，如果莹莹可以送他一些她的阴毛，会让他成为世界上最幸福的男人。

老张把他自己的寄出。其他人也有同样的要求。老张的用完之后，他不得不偷偷从妻子的腋下剪了一些。在一家上海理发店里，老张小心翼翼地把所有的卷发都收了起来。每个人都认为他疯了，只有他自己在偷笑。

这时，老张使出绝招。

“亲爱的，阴毛没有任何意义，我想把自己给你。”

他把全身的裸照寄出去。

吉米疯了，把机票寄给她。

没有得到答复，他写信说他要飞来见她。他当然找不到莹莹，只找到一个邮箱。吉米返回美国并报告了此案。案件发生在海外，当地警方不会认真对待，但吉米却坚持不懈。案件最终移交给了国际刑警组织。

我的侦探朋友被雇了。他确定了吉米的信被寄往哪个邮局，观察并等待了几周。终于有一天，老张来了，打开邮箱，被侦探抓住了。那时候，老张的银行里已经有两百万美元。

法官听了老张的证词，忍不住笑了起来。

由于证据不足，老张无罪释放。

这个圈套成为一个经典的骗局。世界各地的骗子一遍又一遍地复制这个伎俩。即使是现在，在有电子邮件的电脑时代，这个骗局依然流行。

喇嘛

作为香港邵氏兄弟工作室的制片主管，我的工作包括带领重要人物四处参观。

其中有格蕾丝·凯利王妃和摩纳哥王子雷尼尔三世、本尼·希尔、丹尼·凯与他那位全程在责备他的同性妻子等等。

有一天，我听到公关的呼喊："喇嘛来了，喇嘛来了！"

"哪个喇嘛？"我问。

"西藏那里有很多喇嘛。这就是黄袍喇嘛，非常强大。如果他把手放在你的头上，你的余生都会得到祝福！"我可以看到，公关非常兴奋。

一大批豪华轿车抵达。演播室里的每个人都冲向后座，低着头希望能得到祝福。

我见前座的僧人无人理睬，便为他开门。

原来他才是喇嘛，坐在后面的人是当地的僧人。

这位喇嘛是功夫电影的粉丝。我特地为他安排观赏了一场打斗戏，他看得很开心。

我问他中午喜欢吃什么素菜，他回答说："佛陀从来没有说过要远离肉食。他说的是，给你什么你就吃什么。"

我上了一课。

"和尚可以喝酒吗？"

"当我像你这么大的时候，我喝得像条鱼。"

"那么性呢？"我变得大胆，问他。

他平静地回答说："佛教有许多宗派。在我们有更高的理解的状态下，生活没有限制。但是一个人永远、永远不应该伤害其他生物，无论是人类还是蚂蚁。"

“大麻呢？”

“一些藏人用它来接近神。我反对过度使用它。”

“堕胎呢？”

“生死是上天安排的。如果某种情况迫使你别无选择，你会被原谅。”

我深深地鞠了一躬。

“你问了这么多问题，轮到我问你了，”喇嘛说，“你是佛教徒吗？”

“不是，”我谦虚地回答，“希望有一天我会成为其中一员。”

喇嘛微笑着把手放在我的头上。

醉人的早餐

我的母亲生前是一个酒鬼。她早、午、晚都喝白兰地。当我的好朋友倪匡在新加坡拜访我们时，我们给他买了早餐。我点了一桌当地美食。妈妈不知从哪儿掏出一大瓶白兰地，叫倪匡“喝了”！

倪彬彬有礼地说：“但早上喝酒好像有点罪恶感。”

我妈妈冷静地回答：“孩子，巴黎现在是晚上了。”

时间的概念很有趣。

这是发生在东京筑地市场的另一个故事。清晨的时候，你可以在小餐馆里找到最新鲜、最便宜的鱼。这里是鱼贩们辛苦了一夜之后聚集的地方。有一次，我遇到一个酗酒的人，我问他："老头子，你怎么一大早就喝酒了？"

他回答说："年轻人，你为什么晚上喝酒？"

你看，中午或晚上吃龙虾并不稀奇，但如果早上吃，就成了最大的奢侈。星期天早上我总是去鱼市买一只大龙虾当早餐。首先，你将龙虾放在砧板上，然后将一些白醋倒入碗中，再将左手手指浸入其中。这样你就可以抓住龙虾牢牢地不滑走。用一把锋利的刀，砍掉头部并将其切成两半。将头部放入燃烧的木炭中，撒上盐，然后慢慢烧烤。

接下来，把龙虾翻过来。用一把剪刀，把腹部的两边剪下来，把尾巴拿出来。将尾肉垂直切几下，然后将它们切成薄片。把它们扔进一大碗冰水里，看着龙虾肉像花一样盛开。将花朵一一排在盘子上，将红辣椒和绿香菜切小块，像花蕊一样放在中间。将花朵浸入酱油和芥末中，像享用生鱼片一样。

同时，将腿和壳煮成汤，你可以在其中加入豆腐、生菜和任何你喜欢的蔬菜。

当你闻到烤龙虾头的香味时，你就可以吃了！

最后，打开一瓶香槟，播放莫扎特的音乐。

一顿完美的早餐。

与寿司大师周旋

让我们面对现实吧，如果你不是日本人，几乎不可能完全理解如何吃寿司。与厨师交流是欣赏寿司的唯一途径。这就是美食家坚持坐在柜台前与厨师交谈的原因，但如果你不会说他们的语言，这是完全不可能的。这也解释了为什么《米其林指南》给东京餐厅颁发了如此多的星星。不是因为评委知道如何欣赏食物，而是因为更多的寿司厨师会说英语。

当厨师们为他们解释了食物的来源和花了好几年的时间来准备后，这些评委只会哇哇怪叫。

我在日本生活了八年，而且从那以后，每年都继续去那里旅行，我学会了一些如何与第一次见面的寿司大师周旋的技巧。

顾客的“命运”取决于厨师，因为菜单上没有价格。事实上，根本没有菜单。当你结账时，厨师会用他锋利的刀在砧板上划几下。没有固定金额。价格取决于他的心情。

如果他高兴，他就轻砍，当他不高兴时，他就像杀人一样砍，账单变成天文数字。

当然，你可以说我拥有世界上所有的钱并且不在乎，这样你就不会吃到最好的东西，也得不到尊重。我们必须把寿司店当成战场，把厨师当成对手。

“Irasshaimase！”你一进门，厨师就会冲你大喊大叫。这听起来更像是一个挑战而不是欢迎。对此，你轻轻点了点头，“嗯”了一声，仿佛他不存在似的。然后你通过点菜打出第一拳。

“清酒！”你命令。

“Atsukan desuka? Hiyazake desuka?”意思是“热的还是冷的？”他反击。

在这种情况下，你必须通过回答“Nurukan”来再次重击他。这在日语中意味着温暖或室温。顺便说一句，无论是夏天还是冬天，所有最好的清酒都应该这样饮用。

大厨默默点头，感觉到了你不是一个容易对付的对手。

你不能让他休息。看着一大块蛋卷，你点了“Tsumami”，意思是不加米饭。

如果你忘记了这个词，你只需指着说“没有米饭”。大米在日语中也是大米。他会明白的。点寿司只有两种方式：Tsumami或Nigiri。后者的意思是用米饭。

点蛋卷是为了考验寿司师傅的功力。蛋卷是最难完美的。

它是打鸡蛋并在矩形平底锅中一层一层地煎出来的。

在层与层之间，有的师傅放熟虾，有的放鳗鱼。可以加糖和盐。太甜或太咸都会破坏味道。你的对手只能有两种反应。一是他知道——你知道如何欣赏他的食物，但更有可能，他会想：“去你妈的！你在这里有什么好炫耀的？”

如果你看到你的对手面无表情，你必须通过只咬三分之一的蛋卷并保持面无表情来继续战斗。这样他不知道你喜不喜欢。

如果你喜欢昂贵的Uni（海胆）或Awabi（鲍鱼），你的下道菜是点Maguro（金枪鱼的瘦肉部分），而不是Toro（金枪鱼的脂肪部分）。真正的美食家总是欣赏金枪鱼的这种瘦肉部分。日本海捕获的“本金枪鱼”香甜可口，比进口金枪鱼好吃十倍。

仍不确信的厨师会认为他通过给你进口的Maguro来抓住你。你咀嚼了一点，放下它，然后点了Gari（腌姜）。Gari是寿司大师之间的行话，常用于清淡你的味蕾。

现在厨师知道他面对的是什么对手了。在这个精确的时刻，你必须通过点Geso（鱿鱼的煮熟的触手），Odori（在日语中意为跳舞）——来描述活虾，以及Awabi no Wata——鲍鱼的肠子。

厨师从未想过会发生这种情况，他没有时间防守，你可以通过点Tamari（罐底酱油）或Murasaki（在日语中意为紫色，也是酱油的别称）来使出绝招，但从来没有Shoyu，那是俗称。你把生鱼蘸上酱油，然后加一点芥末（绿芥末），在吃之前放在上面。你永远、永远不要在你的酱油中混合芥末，因为这会让它变得浑浊。

你可以随便提一下，在著名作家谷崎润一郎的散文《阴翳礼赞》中，他认为，黑暗物质是多么美丽，它们永远不应该被混合。

这时候你向厨师买了一瓶他们最贵的清酒，吃完三分之二的蛋卷来表达你的感激之情。最后，你喊出“O-iso”，这是账单专用于寿司时的术语。

厨师会恭敬地向你鞠躬，并会给你打折。

味觉调和

我喜欢上海菜。它们混合了咸、甜、油的味道。

“油的我能理解”，朋友说，“但是咸是咸的，甜是甜的，怎么可能又咸又甜呢？”

没有尝过上海菜的人很难体会。

一旦你尝到了它的滋味，你就永远不会厌倦它。

他们的招牌红烧五花肉不仅香甜可口，还混合了猪肉和鱿鱼。

“猪肉就是猪肉，鱿鱼就是鱿鱼，肉和海鲜怎么混？”我的朋友再一次错了。你会发现这个组合非常完美。

为了证明我的观点，澳大利亚菜中最美味的菜肴之一是Carpetbagger。它是通过在一块厚牛排的长边上切一个口制成的。然后在烧烤前插入大量生牡蛎。味道好极了！

应用这一理论，著名的大卫·张在他的百福餐厅做了一道招牌菜。他用红烧猪蹄、生蒜、辣椒酱、味噌和泡菜做配菜，然后用芝麻叶包裹。当然他放了很多生牡蛎。

鹅肝通常与甜果酱一起烹制。

汉字的“鲜”字，左边是“鱼”，右边是羊肉的“羊”。显然，我们的祖先知道。继续发明你自己的菜肴，混合口味和成分。它是有趣的。

一蛋足矣

在保罗·博古斯（Paul Bocuse）去世之前，我见过他好几次。有一次，我在拍摄一个电视旅游节目时，在里昂他的厨房里再次见到了他。

“你能帮我做点东西吗？”我问。

“但我已经很久没有自己做饭了。”他说。

“我不要求任何花哨的东西。只是你每天做的事情。”我要求。

“好吧，看在往日的份上，你想让我做什么？”

我从口袋里拿了东西出来，说：“一个鸡蛋。”

他挠了挠头，但还是答应了。

他拿出一个瓷盘，在上面抹了点油。他用铁夹把盘子放在炉子上。然后他在里面打了一个鸡蛋。他将盘子在火上转动，看着鸡蛋按照自己的喜好烹制。

接着，他把盘子拿出来放在桌子上。

“看！”他说，最后撒一点盐结束表演。

“煮鸡蛋时，每个人都要自己动手。这是通往完美的道路。”

从此，在拍摄众多美食节目时，我会请我遇到的厨师做同样的事情。有一天，我可能会将他们的“特技”编成一本书。

如果有人问我怎么做。我用平底锅，放进去猪油。当我看到猪油冒烟的时候，我把鸡蛋打发，倒进去。我立刻把锅拿走了。剩余的热量会使鸡蛋凝固。只需几滴鱼露即可完成，不需要其他。

这是我做的鸡蛋。

医生大厨

如果你遇到一个法国人，他或她问你：“你在法国哪里吃饭？”你回答巴黎，他们会嗤之以鼻。如果你回答普罗旺斯，他们会说：“当然。”但如果你回答佩里戈尔，他们就会脱帽致敬。

这次旅行是拜访一位老朋友路易斯·穆扎克（Louis Muzac）医生。

佩里戈尔距巴黎四小时火车车程。旅途很舒服。

穆扎克医生带我们去了河边他朋友的餐馆。它俯瞰着一座断桥和一座古老的城堡。一排简单的大白纸灯笼是唯一能营造出童话氛围的装饰。如果你在这种气氛中向你的女朋友求婚，她会答应的。

店主，一个叫丹尼尔·尚邦的中年男子出现了，说：“我不相信米其林星级。我不是厨师，我是一个简单的厨子。”

黑松露和土豆泥。青蛙腿的肉被推到一端，做成一把小伞的形状，然后用黄油烤。你可以把这根小骨头像牙签一样拿起来。

有无数的美食，我不记得了。

“当然，一切都取决于新鲜的当地农产品。”丹尼尔说，揭示了他简单烹饪的秘诀。

第二天早上，我们去穆扎克医生的小屋，上了一堂准备鹅肝酱的课。

在为世人所知之前，鹅肝只是普通家庭主妇制作的传统食品。她们在家里制作并在市场上出售，为自己赚几法郎。穆扎克医生组织了佩里戈尔的家庭主妇，使鹅肝酱的生产成为一个产业。乡下人通过向他提供最好的产品来感谢他。

“首先，我们必须学会如何解剖它。”他说，当然，就像一个真正的医生。

他拿出大块肥美的鹅肝，至少有三公斤重，放在那张旧木桌上。然后他用手术刀将血管一根根取出。

“如果静脉没有被正确去除，鹅肝会很硬。它不会像真正的鹅肝那样光滑。”他说。

他将鹅肝切成手掌大小的块，放入锅中，同时加热猪油。他切碎了一些红葱，然后将它们炸至微微焦糖化。然后他用樱桃酱、红酒和醋来煎鹅肝。

接着，他拿出一大块饼皮，在里面铺上鹅肝片和焦糖红葱。然后他在上面铺上新鲜的黑松露片。这个过程是一层一层地重复的，直到它到达顶部，最后用一块擀好的面皮盖住。把这个大馅饼放进烤箱。

“谁教你这个方法的？”我问。

“我的曾祖父教我的祖父。我的祖父教我的父亲，我的父亲教会了我。我们四代都是外科医生。”

馅饼做好了。我们聚集在旧木桌旁享用。

我必须说这是我一生中吃过的最好的馅饼。

穆扎克医生看着这张桌子回忆道：“二战期间，我就在这张桌子上给士兵做手术。”

完璧之麤皮

2006年，福布斯评选出世界上最贵的三间餐厅：巴黎的Alain Ducasse au Plaza Athénée、伦敦的Restaurant Gordon Ramsay，而排在第一的是位于东京的麤皮。

最好的和牛来自神户。神户是一个没有农场的大城市，那么牛肉从哪里来？每年他们都有一场比赛。邻近农场的所有牛都加入了进来。冠军经常来自三田地区，因此被称为三田牛。

每头小牛都有一张出生证明，上面写着它的父亲和母亲，并附有一个鼻子印。鼻印就像指纹，每头牛都不一样。这里只提供最好的三田牛。

这家餐馆只可招待22位客人。它于1967年开业。除了开放式厨房，没有什么花哨的装饰。这里配备了巨大的备前（地名，属于日本冈山县）炭炉，烧烤炉从餐厅开业就在。

这里没有菜单。先上的是开胃菜，可供选择的食物有野生三文鱼、肥美的鳗鱼、最新鲜的虾或轻烤鲍鱼。沙拉里拌着海胆。

你的牛排要几分熟？通常可以点两分熟、五分熟或全熟。

这家餐厅为你提供十种烧烤选择：

1. 一分熟。

2. 两分熟。

3. 三分熟。

4. 四分熟。

5. 半熟。

6. 六分熟。

7. 七分熟。

8. 八分熟。

9. 九分熟。

10. 全熟。

如果是一群人去，建议点几种烤肉来分享。通过这种方式，你可以享受和比较它们精致的味道。

对于“一分熟”的，你可以像切黄油一样用热刀切。要完美地烤制它，外层要烤焦，以密封里面的汁液，没有发现血迹。很神奇。

西冷牛排和菲力牛排有什么区别？前者的顶端有一块圆圆的肥肉，我喜欢它。

这里拥有最长的酒单。每一口罗曼尼·康帝都不一样，搭配三田牛是好的选择。

当经理来问我的意见时，我说“完璧（Kanpeki）”，这是日语中完美的意思。

黑泽明餐厅

如果你喜欢日本电影和日本牛肉，但又不想支付飍皮的价格，我建议你去黑泽明餐厅。

这是他的家族经营的。

在筑地市场的一座两层木屋里，你可以在一条小巷子里找到它，这里曾经是旧鱼市。这座建筑曾经是一座艺妓院，是艺妓生活的地方。

当你进去的时候，你会看到一幅黑泽明本人的巨大肖像。菜单的设计和印刷就像电影剧本。

墙上挂着黑泽明导演的所有电影的照片。喜欢他电影的朋友可以一一浏览。

烹饪是按照他喜欢的方式来做的。

一份晚餐大约需要180美元，其中包括龙虾或鲍鱼等开胃小菜。然后是牡蛎汤，主菜是厚厚的铁板烧和牛牛排，最后是日本蜜瓜。

牛排在你面前煮熟，厨师会根据你的喜好准备，你只需要提出就可以了。没有低俗的炫技，只有优秀的传统烧烤。如果你还饿，厨师会用很多大蒜瓣来炒饭。这是一顿值得纪念的饭。

位于东京国会大厦附近的另一家黑泽明餐厅则提供日本面条。日本人去面馆不是为了面条，而是为了清酒。在这里可以喝到很多牌子的清酒。还可以用合理的价格享用寿喜烧（一种用汤煮的牛肉片）和其他种类的日本料理。试试吧。

你甚至可能会在那里看到以武士鬼魂的形式出现的黑泽明。

猪油

我很喜欢吃猪油拌饭，以至于我不得不在香港开设自己的餐厅。我妈妈一直用猪油做饭，我是吃猪油长大的！制作猪油，她用了一大块五花肉，切成一寸见方的肉块，放在平底锅里煎。油从脂肪里面渗出来，留下酥脆的猪油渣给孩子们分享。我们永远等不及它们冷却下来，因为它们闻起来很香。我们大把大把地嚼，直到我们舌头灼伤，喉咙痛。战后，我们都很穷，一碗猪油拌饭就是天下美味。

时代变了。现在人人都用植物油，因为猪油被贴上了“不健康”的标签。它已经成为我们日常生活中的有害物。没有一家餐厅敢用它。饭菜越来越不好吃了，但没有人抱怨。

当我们去一家法国餐馆时，他们给了我们面包和牛油（黄油）。因为食物上桌需要很长时间，所以我们吃了很多牛油填饱了肚子，毫不畏惧地把牛油堆在面包上。后来我们发现牛油对我们身体的危害比猪油还大。

医学研究证明，猪油富含健康所需的单不饱和脂肪。其中大部分是油酸，与橄榄油中的健康物质相同。

不吃猪油的人可能从未洗过盘子。如果他们像我一样经常洗碗，他们会惊讶地发现猪油比植物油更容易洗掉。

在我去过的所有地方，人们都吃猪油渣。它们在拉丁国家被称为“Chicharrónes”。在魁北克，它们被称为“Oreilles de Christ”或“Christ’s Ear”。如果你到法国的乡村酒吧，调酒师会给你“Graton”。在南斯拉夫，他们会给你“Čvarci”。我爱意大利人，他们把整块纯猪油变成意大利腊肠！在湄公河地区，泰国北部的人们离不开 Khaep Mu：糯米和猪皮。

我的餐厅英文名叫“胆固醇万岁”（中文名：“粗菜馆”）。

猪油爱好者都在这里聚集。三十年来没有变化。

我尊重那些因为宗教信仰而不吃猪肉的人，但我爱猪油。

欣赏中国诗

中国诗歌有多种形式。一种常见的叫绝句。它是一个四行诗，一组四行。第一、二、四行以押韵结尾，例如：

横看成岭侧成峰，

远近高低各不同。

不识庐山真面目，

只缘身在此山中。

还有一个是这样的：

终日昏昏醉梦间，

忽闻春尽强登山。

因过竹院逢僧话，

又得浮生半日闲。

这首诗也可以反过来读：

又得浮生半日闲，

因过竹院逢僧话。

忽闻春尽强登山，

终日昏昏醉梦间。

还有一种禅诗的第一句和最后一句相同：

庐山烟雨浙江潮，

未到千般恨不消。

到得还来别无事，

庐山烟雨浙江潮。

欣赏中国画

中国画从来就不是写实的。它们是写意的，题材总是一样的。同样的山，同样的树，同样的河流，它们可能相当乏味。总是画在一个垂直长方框里，很少是正方形，也很少横的。重点是练习用不同的方式画每一个物体，并记住它们。当你创作一幅画时，你会根据你的想象，把它们都放在一个方框里。这并不取决于你如何用眼睛去看它们，而是取决于你如何在脑海中想象它们。在顶部总有一片空白，让你的想象力尽情驰骋，这是你走向无限的旅程的起点。

好，让我们走进一幅中国画。首先，你看到一条河，然后有一条船。有两个人影刚上岸。一个是书生，也就是你自己，另一个是替你背包袱的书童。

人物非常小，只是为了显示山有多高，森林有多深。当你爬上山路时，你会欣赏每棵树的不同之处。

树叶的颜色告诉你，画里的季节。当你继续登山，会看到瀑布。看到流水凉爽而清澈，你坐在一块岩石上休息。无须吩咐，书童就拿出一个小火炉、一些木炭和一个陶罐准备泡茶。喝了几杯之后，你又开始了你的旅程。

也许沿路有一幢大宅，可能是一幢满是漂亮妓女的房子。你被她们逗乐了。对像你这样的书生来说，跟学音乐、诗歌和舞蹈的女士们在一起是多么愉快啊，这些都是你妻子所缺乏的。酒后微醺，你已经到达山顶。

在云海中，你看到一只巨大的丹顶鹤。你骑着它，飞向无限。

生活充实，人就有信心

学习

当你旅行时，你会学到很多哲理。

我在印度丛林拍摄的时候，我们发现那里的大多数人都是素食主义者。由于我们是外宾，我们偶尔会吃鸡肉，但从不吃鱼。三个月过去了，没有吃到一条鱼，我想得要命。

“你能给我煮点鱼吗？”我问负责做菜的老太太。

“什么是鱼？”她问。

“鱼是世界上最好吃的东西！”我拿出一张纸，在上面画了一条鱼。

“如果你没有吃过，那真是太可惜了。”我怜悯地看了她一眼。

“可是先生，”她说，“如果你一开始就没有吃过，怎么会可惜呢？”

我在伊比沙岛拍摄的时候，去海滩散步。水很清澈，可以看到鱼在游动。

我看到附近有一位年迈的嬉皮士在钓鱼。他面前的鱼很小，而我身边的鱼却很大。

“过来，老伙计，”我说，“这里有更大的鱼！”

老嬉皮抬起头，笑道：“可是我钓的只是早餐呀。”

离别

我去过泰姬陵很多次。很多年前我去那里的时候，从孟买出发要坐五六个小时的车。现在你可以直接飞到陵墓所在的阿格拉。

你跟随一长队的游客，慢慢地到达大门，这是一个完全黑暗的巨大圆顶。然后，轰！突然间，你会看到这座巨大的白色大理石建筑就在你面前。不止一个，而是两个！另一个是水面上的倒影。这会给你留下难以忘怀的印象。

相传沙贾汗皇帝为他心爱的妻子建造了这座坟墓，并想和她一起下葬。这是假的！如果你有时间仔细探索阿格拉，你会在附近发现另一座未完工的坟墓。它是黑色的！皇帝想为自己造一座黑色大理石墓。

不管怎样，我们不是来上历史课的。如果你喜欢这个故事，你可以百度一下。

第三次到访时，我从早上一直待到黄昏。当我惊叹于夕阳将泰姬陵变成金色时，我的向导告诉我：“如果你在满月时看，它会更加美丽。”

我看了一下农历，刚好是十五。

“我去吃晚饭再回来。”我对我的向导说。

当我回来的时候，我看到满月正从泰姬陵后面升起。这使得建筑变得半透明。

这是我一生中见过的最令人印象深刻的景象！

我不想离开。

“虽然它很漂亮，但它仍然是一座坟墓。夫妻一起看满月是不吉利的。他们注定要分开。”我想，如果你深深爱着一个人，但出于某种原因，你不得不离开对方，在满月的时候把你的爱人带到泰姬陵，让导游讲述这个故事。

他或她会理解你，一切都会被原谅。

巴塞罗那240俱乐部

我们和三十名香港特技演员一起到达巴塞罗那，他们中没有一个人会说西班牙语。他们都血气方刚，过了几天就开始变得焦躁不安。

“帮帮我们！”他们说。作为制片人和摄制组的负责人，我必须解决大大小小的问题。

“在旅馆后面有很多流莺。”我回答道。

“但是安全吗？”

“我怎么会知道？”

“这仍然不能解决我们的问题。”

然后我想起了我在飞机上遇到的一个人，他给了我他的名片。上面写着“Club 240 Dos Cuarenta”。

我把它给了其中一位特技演员：“这里可能有你们需要的。”

“这只是迪斯科呀！”他看着卡片抗议道。

“不完全是。”我解释说给我名片的人是老板。他说那也是一家妓院，里面所有的女孩都会说英语。

“我们试试吧。”其中一个特技演员说。

“怎么样？”第二天见到他们时，我问道。

“超棒！简直是一个天堂。”他们明显变得轻松。

这引起了我的好奇：“妓院就是妓院。这个有什么特别的？”

特技演员详细给我描绘。

“当我们坐出租车到达时，我们看到一大群人，男人和女人都在排队买票。我们走进去，看见一大群人在跳舞。有许多漂亮的女孩坐在沙发上。

“她们都很友好，所以我们开始和她们交谈。如果你觉得太吵了，你可以去客厅的另一边，那里有柔和的拉丁音乐。

"我们看到给你名片的人了，他认出我们来了。我们问他为什么那里的女士都那么漂亮。他说他有外面的保镖来管控质量。"

我忍不住笑出来。

特技演员开始告诉我们更多。他说，男孩在这里遇到女孩。他们商定了价格，然后去附近的酒店。这种经营方式多聪明！老板不必负责女孩的医疗保险。他只通过收取入场费和饮料来赚钱。

当女孩们短聚后回来，必须再次付费才能进入。如果我们去普通迪斯科和女孩聊天，我们可能会被对方拒绝。但在240俱乐部绝对不会。

我们像穿着闪亮盔甲的骑士一样被对待。这是获得自信的绝妙方法！

的确，做生意的方法无数。

曼德勒之路

我从不喜欢乘坐豪华邮轮。那些容纳数千人的新船。所有的房间都一样。每个人都冲到自助餐厅吃冷冻牛排，有时是冷冻龙虾，没有什么是新鲜的。

表演节目的都是二三流艺人。宾果游戏会让你变成一个老人。几天后你会感到恶心和疲倦。

小船会好一点，就像那些穿越希腊群岛的小邮轮。每艘船都有自己的特点。塔希提岛的邮轮也很棒，高更（Gauguin）到过的每个地方都有一个停靠点。

我最难忘的乘船之旅叫作“曼德勒之路”，从蒲甘出发的一条内陆河游轮。它是缅甸最豪华的游轮之一。法国人称他们在东南亚的前殖民地为印度支那。这个名字本身听起来充满异国情调和诗意。

登上这艘船的那一刻，你会发现河流如丝绸般光滑。在这次旅行中，你永远不会晕船。

粉红色的日落和金黄色的日出。每天早晨，你都会在河边宝塔的锣声中醒来。早餐和正餐是热带水果和当地特色的盛宴。你可以上岸参观许多古老的寺庙，这些都可以在明信片上找到。你必须亲身感受的是当地人。

首先，你永远不会遇到像你在印度和东南亚其他地区看到的乞丐。为什么？之后你就会发现，如果一个人饿了，可以去缅甸的任何寺庙，那里都会有食物。食物来自普通人。给僧人送饭是缅甸人一生中最幸福的事。当然，僧侣不可能吃完所有的食物，剩下的食物会分给任何需要的人。

在漆黑的夜晚也有节目娱乐。其中一个节目被称为“惊喜”。如果有大雨或暴风雨，则无法进行。

如果幸运的话，你可能会看到一颗星星向你走来。然后是两颗，然后是三颗，然后是无数。满天星星。在你的生活中，你不可能近距离看到这么多星星。这是梦幻的。

我发现船上的所有船员都乘坐小艇逆流而上。在那里，船员点燃了数千支蜡烛，并将蜡烛放在香蕉叶制成的小船上，蜡烛像星星般，顺着河水流向我们，创造出这种梦幻的效果。

这是一个你永远不会忘记的迷人景象。

惩罚

在萨格勒布拍摄电影时，我们周日休息。与我成为好朋友的当地特技演员问道："为什么不和我一起到维也纳？我可以开车送你过去。"

"维也纳？我一直想去那里。我听过很多关于这座音乐之都的故事。"

"那我们走吧。"他催促道。

"可是我们只有一天的假期，离这里还有多远？"

"一般人开车要四个小时。我们是特技演员，开车三小时就能到。我们可以早点出发，当天晚上就能回来。"

他的建议听起来很诱人，我同意了。

星期天他来接我。他带着他的妻子。

“左转！向右转！……”我发现她是后座司机。不仅如此，她还是个话痨，一路说个不停。

我闭上眼睛睡觉。

突然，我被警察摩托车的警报器声吵醒了。

特技演员把车停在了人行道。他的妻子开始对他大喊大叫：“我告诉过你不要开这么快！看你给我们惹了什么麻烦……”

警察上前。妻子继续抱怨。

“你从来不听我的。永远是你，你，你！你知道我们要付多少罚款吗？……”

“我可以知道你和这位女士之间的关系吗？”警察问道。

“她是我的妻子，”特技演员回答。

“几年了？”

“二十年。”

警察合上了他的票簿。他向特技演员敬了个礼说：“先生，你可以走了。你已经受到了足够的惩罚。”

世界上最幸福的国家？

经常和我一起旅行的朋友们是“安缦迷”，之所以这么命名，是因为他们爱上了这个酒店集团，发誓要入住这个集团的每一家酒店。

除了不丹，还有什么地方可以找到更多的“安缦”？

联合国的一项调查显示，不丹人是世界上最幸福的人。为了追寻乌托邦，我们从香港飞过曼谷，在达卡停留加油，最后降落在帕罗。

空气没有人们说的那么稀薄。我们在这个高山国家呼吸没有问题。应该担心的是晕车，因为所有的道路都是崎岖不平的。不丹唯一平坦的道路，肯定是机场的跑道。我们住的第一间安缦，是在不丹首都廷布。导游说是半小时的路程，但到那里用了两个小时。

不丹的所有安缦都有一个共同点，那就是你永远无法直接看到这座建筑，必须穿过一条美丽的山路，上坡下山才能到达那里。所有的建筑材料都是天然的，并在当地找到。排列坚固的石头以形成庭院。地板上覆盖着从附近森林砍下的松木。不丹有一条法律，砍伐一棵树，必须种植三棵树。

房间很宽敞，床很软。墙上有一个大炉子，你想烧多少松木就烧多少。中央有一个大浴缸。除了没有电视或任何现代电器外，一切都装备精良。你从未在任何安缦见过这些。我们睡得很好，早上，阳光透过窗框照进来，投下的阴影就像梵文经文。三餐都包括在内，我们可以吃西餐、印度餐或泰餐。食物没什么可评论的，我们不是去米其林餐厅。不丹是干旱国家的传言是不真实的。

酒吧里有当地的白兰地或威士忌可供选择，但只有啤酒很好。这最好的一个叫二万一（Twenty-One Thousand）。

下一个目的地是岗提。想到崎岖不平的道路，我问向导需要多少小时。他说“六个小时”。这意味着至少需要九个小时，实际上需要十个小时。

景色相当单调。“砍一植三”的法律在这里行不通，我看到的大部分山都是光秃秃的。岗提在一个山谷里。我们经过了许多有很多鱼的溪流。你需要许可证才能捕鱼。不丹人不鼓励杀生，所以他们自己也不吃鱼。那天晚上在酒店，我们吃了专门从印度进口给游客的冷冻鱼。

我们向北搬到了普纳卡。普纳卡安缦是由一座古老的寺庙重建而成。我们不得不过一座吊桥，然后再转乘高尔夫球车才能到达。和岗提那间一样，也只有八间房，面积却大了三倍。

最令人难忘的观光景点是普纳卡堡。它建于1635年，经历了多次地震和火灾。

寺庙的佛像非常巨大。数以千计的红袍僧人在锣鼓声中齐心协力。这是惊心动魄的，有那么一刻你能感觉到佛的存在。

参观完寺庙之后，我们去野餐。

安缦酒店会把一切安排妥当，英式篮子配有瓷盘和水晶玻璃杯。食物非常好，要是没有苍蝇就好了！

不丹是一个多山的国家。普通人住在哪里？当然是在山上。由于没有办法用卡车运来建筑材料，只能由工人搬运。随着电视的到来，人们接触到先进社会的美好事物，渴望住进平坦的现代公寓中。房地产开发商蜂拥而至，但他们不得不遵守一项规定，要求所有公寓的门窗都必须是不丹风格的。这造成了不平衡的外观，我认为这很丑陋。

我们回到机场所在的帕罗。帕罗安缦位于深山中。你必须走很长的路才能到达入口。通往那里的小路被厚厚的松针覆盖，走起来柔软舒适。到那里我拿出一包包方便面，请酒店厨师烹调。他尝试了一口，立即被迷住了。

回到帕罗的主要原因是攀登“虎巢”。你可以骑一头驴到其中一座山上。但要达到顶峰，你必须自己爬两座高山。一路爬上去，看到景色后，朋友们可能会问：“值得吗？”历尽千辛万苦，你当然会点头回答：“是的！”

我遇到了一位不丹妇女，她正背着她蹒跚学步的孩子回家。她大概已经在稻田里工作了一整天。她抬头看着她家所在的小山，长路漫漫。她脸上的表情不是高兴，而是深深的无奈。

我应该在我年轻的时候来不丹。那个年代，一切都是美好的。

马丘比丘杂谈

从香港飞往迪拜的午夜航班需要八个小时，然后等待中转需要四个小时，之后需要十六个小时的航程才能到达圣保罗，最后还需要三个小时飞往秘鲁首都利马。这是一段漫长的旅程。

那里有大型美国连锁酒店，但我们不感兴趣。我们在米拉弗洛雷斯的一家优雅的酒店安顿下来。

第一件事：购物。还有什么比在秘鲁购买Vicuña[①]更好的呢？Vicuña被称为“神的纤维”，它是世界上最好的羊毛之一，仅次于藏羚羊的羊毛。由于“沙图什”（Shahtoosh）[②]被WTO禁止贸易，Vicuña是用钱能买到的最好的产品。每年Vicuña[③]被成群地放牧并用古柯叶喂养。这是为了让动物们在剪毛时保持平静和愉悦。

为什么Vicuña这么特别？人的头发直径是30微米，而Vicuña的直径只有11.7微米！最长的毛在腹部，但脖子上的毛才是珍贵的。专门从事高端羊毛产品的意大利公司Loro Piana很早以前就知道这一点，并与秘鲁政府达成了交易。当时收集的羊毛被运回意大利加工，最终产品将在两者之间分享，一小部分卖给日本公司Nisikawa。

在利马，你会发现Vicuña围巾的价格仅为Loro Piana的三分之一！

我们去了一家名为Panchita的餐厅，它被誉为利马最好的餐厅。在那里，我看到每个人都拿着深粉色的饮料。我当然也跟着点

---

① 骆马毛，下文未特殊标注均为此意。——编者注

② 用藏羚羊绒毛制成的披肩。——编者注

③ 骆马。——编者注

了。它由紫玉米和一些香料混合橙汁制成。相当不错！当你去到利马，一定不要错过。食物主要是烧烤，其中一道主菜是用香蕉叶包裹的猪肉和红薯，非常好吃。

第二天早上，我们坐了两个小时的飞机飞往库斯科。它海拔4000米，当我们着陆时，我感到有点头晕。

当地导游让我喝点古柯。我们在机场找到了一家商店，那里有一个很大的招牌，上面写着“Coca”，在那里显然是完全合法的。店主抓起一把干古柯叶，放在杯子里，然后倒热水给我们泡茶。

嗯，在秘鲁时，就像在罗马时一样，我喝了古柯茶。但这对我完全没有作用。

另一家商店出售古柯茶包，这让我很反感。在接下来的几天里，我尝试咀嚼生古柯叶，但结果是一样的。也许他们向游客出售的是其他茶叶。

库斯科是印加王朝的古都。据说街道是用黄金铺成的，但西班牙人把它全部拿走了。

大多数人直接从这里前往马丘比丘，但我们不赶时间，我们在一个叫作圣谷的地方停了下来。很难想象这样一个天堂，在海拔4000米处满是奇花异草。天空是蓝色的，一望无际的蓝色让我屏住呼吸。

妇女们带着纪念品一路上到这座高山上供游客购买。你根本无法拒绝她们。有数百种不同的斗篷。你怎么只选一个？很简单，和选择领带一样。当你走进商店时，货架上有成千上万的商品，你感到困惑，就选择第一个吸引你眼球的。

第二天早上，我饿醒了。长桌上摆着很多水果，作为早餐。有很多种百香果是我从未见过的。我一向认为百香果是酸的。不过在这里，它们像蜂蜜一样甜。

主要食物当然是藜麦。几个世纪以来，秘鲁人一直在吃这个。田野里长满了这种开花植物。

直到宇航员将藜麦带到太空并且健康爱好者将其作为主食的一部分，它才变得昂贵。

我们到了火车站。有一列蓝色火车在等我们。它由运营东方快车的公司运营。

它仍然保留着旅行黄金时代的优雅的亚麻桌布、银器、水晶香槟杯和所有你能享受到的美食体验。火车一路把我们带到马丘比丘。

从山脚下出发还有四十分钟的巴士车程。这条路是如此曲折和危险，让我想起了伊夫·蒙当（Yves Montana）的电影《恐惧的代价》（*The Wages of Fear*）。我们到达了马丘比丘的大门。我首先看到的是不少游客在呕吐。我们带着行李，心急地赶往目的地。爬上几座山头，整个城镇的废墟就在眼前。我想知道这些巨大的石头是如何被抬到这个偏远的山顶上的，它们是如何排列得如此完美的。一定是外星人教了印加人！我估计，在它的辉煌时期，这座城市一定有成千上万的人居住。

“只有 750人，”导游似乎读懂了我的想法，“只有牧师和他们的家人被允许住在这里。普通人每天都得爬上去。”

“他们为什么选择这座山？”

“传说很多，但没有一个得到证实。”

“也许是为了躲避洪水？”我只能想到简单的答案。

“有趣的想法。”导游说。

那天晚上，天空布满了星星。我想到了不明飞行物和入侵者。

是时候离开了。我们回到了库斯科和文明中。

Palacio Nazarenas酒店是我住过的最令人印象深刻的酒店之一。床很大，浴室和现代酒店套房一样大。地板被加热了。多年来我从未睡得这么安稳。第二天早上，我发现除了空调，酒店还向房间里输送氧气。

享用了丰盛的早餐后，我们参观了旅馆。有一个私人小教堂，墙上挂满了画。所有的圣经故事都有记载。我看着那些画里的人物，我发誓我以前见过他们。那是博特罗作品中的红红的、圆滚滚的脸。

看起来他比我们先到了……

三十年威士忌配百万年的冰

我们从秘鲁前往布宜诺斯艾利斯，阿根廷的首都。

我的第一印象是，这里的林荫大道是世界上最宽的。市中心，每边十车道。它需要一个独裁者驱逐所有居民才能实现。

阿根廷首都号称小巴黎，但灯火阑珊，气氛阴沉。它远没有你想象的那么浪漫。不要为我哭泣。

我们住在四季酒店。当地导游说他们的牛排馆是最好的。肉的确很大块，每一块肉都和得克萨斯T骨牛排一样大。服务员从来没有问过你想要几分熟，每一块都是全熟，很好，非常非常耐嚼。

肉本身很好，至少我的朋友说。我想如果它很好，它应该作为最好的鞑靼牛排。当我向服务员提议，他看着我，好像我是个野蛮人！在接下来的几天里，我们吃了一份又一份的牛排，从街头小摊到最昂贵的餐馆。它们都硬得要命。

请原谅我对阿根廷牛排缺乏欣赏。如果你想要味道丰富的牛排，你应该在纽约尝试彼得·鲁格（Peter Luger）的熟成牛排。如果你想要柔软的、嫩的，你应该尝试日本三田和牛。我这样说是没有偏见的。

阿根廷的一种让我难忘的味道是他们的国饮马蒂。它是由冬青叶制成的。每个人都从一个像橙子大小的小碗里喝它。它是在朋友之间共享的，喝完了可以再加热水。味道很特别，我真的很喜欢。

我们在一家名为La Brigadas的著名餐厅用餐。墙上贴满了著名足球队的徽章。

领班不是用刀而是用勺子切大块牛排来炫耀。当隔壁桌的美国游客拍手时，我摸到了勺子的边缘，这是你能找到的最锋利的刀片！他们最好的葡萄酒是D.V. Catena和Catena Zapata，都来自马尔贝克。它们就像匈牙利公牛血一样烈。

晚饭后我们去跳探戈。对任何到阿根廷的人来说，这是必须做的事。舞厅里挤满了像我们这样的业余跳舞游客，而不是阿根廷人。

离开大城市后，我们前往埃尔卡拉法特（El Calafate）看冰川。

小船向着冰层驶去。首先你看到了一大块冰。然后更多。你最终得到了一个像岛屿一样大的东西。它是蓝色的。不是普通的蓝色，而是像海军蓝墨水一样的深蓝色。有数百座这样的蓝山向我们走来。

船长停止了引擎。他用一根长杆，巧妙地勾住了附近的一大块冰川。他把它切成块，然后把这些冰块放入威士忌酒杯里。我们将三十年的苏格兰威士忌倒入百万年的冰中。

这是我喝过的最令人满意的饮料之一。

如果你认为这座冰川很大，那么与佩里托莫雷诺最大的冰川比比，后者的面积是267平方英里①！

长长的木制平台围绕冰川建造，因此可以近距离观看。就好像

---

① 1平方英里约2.6平方公里。——编者注

天是冰，地也是冰。

我们乘坐飞机从上面看佩里托莫雷诺冰川。原来那是一条大河，流入大海，在那里遇到冷空气，就结冰了。我们从天空看到的冰川只有一颗麦粒那么小。

我们旅程的最后一站是伊瓜苏瀑布。我们飞越了比亚马孙大得多的无边丛林。一条大河穿过它。在河口处，水流变窄，形成许多瀑布从悬崖上直泻而下。

“看起来不大。”我说。

“等我们着陆。”飞行员喊道。

世界上最大的瀑布是位于赞比亚和津巴布韦边界的维多利亚瀑布，其次是尼亚加拉瀑布和伊瓜苏瀑布。伊瓜苏被岩石隔开，使尼亚加拉看起来是第二大的。但伊瓜苏比尼亚加拉高出三倍。犹如千龙从天而降。这是人一生必去的地方。

用埃莉诺·罗斯福（Eleanor Roosevelt）在看到伊瓜苏后的话来说：“可怜的尼亚加拉！”

追寻高更

我喜欢高更的画作和萨默塞特·毛姆（Somerset Maugham）的小说。我发誓要去塔希提岛，有一天我做到了。

我登上了一艘名为“保罗·高更”的小船，船停在画家保罗·高更曾经去过的岛屿。塔希提岛是法属波利尼西亚最大的岛屿，但人口只有13万。

除了湛蓝的大海和椰子树，没有什么可看的。顺便说一下，并非所有椰子的味道都一样。我都试过了，发现只有泰国椰子是最好的。面包果树随处可见。果实有篮球那么大。当地人把它们切成块，用椰子油煎炸或磨成面粉烘烤。有人说它尝起来像土豆，但我觉得它很平淡。淀粉是这里的主食。每个人都像高更的画上的一样矮胖。我经过一所学校，发现没有一个人瘦。

一些法国人移民到这些岛屿，与当地的女士结婚并定居下来。他们开了法国餐馆，相当不错。当你在那里时，你应该尝试一家叫作“Le Coco’s”的餐馆。

我去了高更博物馆。一切画作都是复制品，但你仍然可以在那里了解他的生活轨迹。我买了一块印有《两个女人》的布，直到今天一直在夏天用它作为纱笼。纱笼不容易缠在腰上。你可以买一个鲍鱼壳做的扣子，防止它掉下来。

是时候登船前往其他岛屿了。船长给了每个人一瓶香槟。威士忌和白兰地可以随意饮用。餐点是“西餐”，与法国或意大利的没有什么不同。如果你不喜欢和其他人一起吃饭，你可以享受24小时客房服务。

有无数的日出和日落值得观看。

我们接下来停在了胡阿希内岛——库克船长发现的一个岛屿。法国人不仅将他们的文化带到了这个岛上，还带来了他们的核弹试验。岛上开满了芙蓉花。每个人的耳朵后面都塞了一个红色的。我也这样做了。到处都是养鱼场。巨大的鳗鱼被当作宠物而不是食物饲养。

船在午夜再次航行。

我们到达了波拉波拉岛。詹姆斯·米切纳有句名言："每个去过那里的人都想回去。"现在我们真的在南太平洋了。它是最美丽的，也是真正的天堂。难怪二战后美国士兵来到这个岛上休养。

我们去了一望无际的白色柔软沙滩进行野餐和"摸鱼"。我们的水手将面包屑扔进清澈的水中，一群鲨鱼聚集在一起。不要担心。我们吃了它们的鳍，但它们从来没有吃过我们的腿。我们可以潜入大海去触摸它们。它们似乎很高兴。鲨鱼之后是刺鳐。它们会成群结队地包围你。你可以翻转它们来抚摸它们的白色肚子。它们并不介意。

回到船上，你可以观看绿色闪光。我们中很少有人见过它，也没有拍照。这是一种视错觉。如果你看一会儿落日，它会在你的眼球上形成一个偏差，其他的光线将被过滤掉，让一切都变成绿色。我试了试。我看见太阳变成了又大又圆的一块玉。

我们错过了参观马龙·白兰度（Marlon Brando）的岛的机会。他写道，当台风来临时，它吹了七天七夜。如果他死在那个岛上，人们将永远记住他，他是《叛舰喋血记》中的船长，一个年轻英俊的人，不是又老又胖。

接下来，我们来到塔哈岛，它也被称为香草岛。我们学会了如何种植这种植物。那里的香草非常便宜，你会想买很多来做几加仑的冰淇淋。

最后一个岛叫莫雷阿岛。那里的主要生意是卖黑珍珠。我问了一个非常愚蠢的问题："为什么世界上其他地方的珍珠是白色的，而塔希提岛的珍珠是黑色的？"

"因为我们的牡蛎是黑色的。"显而易见的答案。

是时候回家了。

米切纳是对的。我想再来。

时光流逝

如果你喜欢电影，你不会错过经典的《卡萨布兰卡》。卡萨布兰卡（Casa Blanca），这是一个刻在我脑海中的名字。当我还是个孩子的时候，我就迷上了，从那时起就想参观这个地方。最后，我和"安缦迷"一起上路了。

我们是怎么到那里的？首先，搭乘航班飞往迪拜，然后再飞八小时，降落在卡萨布兰卡。当然，Casa的意思是房子，Blanca的意思是白色。我们没有看到它们。这座摩洛哥最大的城市，古老又残缺。

我们直接去了使小镇闻名的Rick’s Café。据说一切都是按照电影场景重建的，但实际上却大不相同。甚至他们演奏*As Time Goes By*的钢琴也没有放在正确的位置。卡萨布兰卡原本没有Rick’s Café，直到一位在大使馆工作的美国女士退休并想出重新创建它的主意。这条消息发布在社交媒体上，全世界影迷纷纷捐款。这座电影爱好者的圣地于2004年竣工，此后一直蓬勃发展。

嗯，那里的食物还不错，但是干马提尼不干。没有汉弗莱·博加特（Humphrey Bogart），也没有英格丽·褒曼（Ingird Bergman）落入他的怀抱。我们不得不发挥我们的想象力。

街头食品既便宜又有趣。小贩带着一大批当地面包来了，顾客们试图用手指选择最大的。不适合卫生、胆小或注重健康的女士，但我不在乎。我点了一个，小贩切面包，切一个煮熟的鸡蛋。然后他加了奶酪。我以为是本地产品，但仔细一看，原来是法国的乐芝牛。

最好的餐厅叫作Café Maure。穿过蓝色的门，就可以看到一排排的民族厨具Tajine。肉类和蔬菜在这个黏土容器中慢慢煮熟。你可以点到任何你喜欢吃的东西。我发现鸡肉很无味，但羊肉很棒！有一种叫作“大使”的饮料。它由甜枣、杏仁和牛奶制成。必须尝试。

第二天，我们飞往马拉喀什，这是一个沙漠小镇的真实例子。

我相信每个人都在纪录片中看过它的夜市，但直到你在那里，你才能感受到它的浩瀚。有无穷无尽的食物供我们选择。我们吃了烤羊脑、牛内脏、从未见过的贝类。如果你有一个强大的胃，你会没事的。如果没有，想都不要想！最好的用餐地点是屋顶上的咖啡馆，可以俯瞰无数的摊位。告诉服务员你喜欢什么，他会拿过来给你。

进出这个世界上最大的夜市时，可能很难屏住呼吸。但是一定要试一试，因为马和驴的排泄物的刺鼻气味可能会让你心烦意乱。

你能想象在沙漠中种植玫瑰吗？自古以来，马拉喀什一直是沙漠中的瑰宝。一切都在这里繁荣昌盛。你可以扔一颗枣子，它很快就会长成一棵树。玫瑰园是惊人的！那里的人爱它们。

我们住在安缦的Amanjena，一个以沙漠小屋风格设计的度假村。这些房间被称为“亭子”，一共有三十二间。比安缦最初规划的最多三十间房，多了两间。酒店四周环绕着清澈的水池。沙漠中还有什么比水更奢侈的呢？

第二天我们去购物了。大多数纪念品可以在其他地方买到，但摩洛哥坚果油不在此列。《纽约时报》称，它是世界上最好的抗衰老油。自从他们发表了一篇关于它的文章以来，每个人都蜂拥而至购买。

我买的另一件东西是Djellaba。这是一件带兜帽的长袍。在我穿上它之后，朋友说我长得像邓布利多教授。当地人向我微笑，因为我尊重他们的文化。

老城区中心的咖啡馆，叫作Le Jardin，是个休息的好地方。晚餐在Al Fassia餐厅享用，该餐厅拥有种满大黄玫瑰的花园。由全女性团队运营，她们为我们做了美味的家常菜。我认为最好的选择是甜鸽肉煎饺。我强烈建议你试试。

我们现在与《卡萨布兰卡》的距离只差了钢琴和钢琴师萨姆。

是人，不是地方

如果我们谈论《卡萨布兰卡》，那么真正的白房子只能在希腊找到。在那里，人们使用了一种由粉状白色石头制成的油漆，它不会变脏，并可以让墙壁保持多年的白色光亮。屋顶是蓝色的，以增强美感。这种建筑在所有希腊岛屿上随处可见，给人留下难忘的印象。

我们的旅程从首都雅典开始。

我们登上了一艘名为Tere Moana的船，因为我们在前往塔希提岛时很喜欢她的姊妹船Paul Gauguin。

它停在所有怪物般大的邮轮所无法停靠的小岛上。我们住的酒店俯瞰雅典卫城。日出和日落使它更加雄伟。人们永远不会厌倦欣赏它。

小镇虽然在山顶，但我们可以打车上去看看。柱子保存完好。

希腊政府不遗余力地恢复和清理它们，使其恢复昔日的辉煌。很难想象它建于公元前6世纪。难怪它被罗马人、现代欧洲人和美国人复制。

然而，观察希腊人现在的生活方式很有趣。每天都有罢工。人们即使罢工也能得到报酬，所以他们很乐意继续罢工。为了赢得选票，政党给人们额外的假期，公民现在每周只需要工作三天半。难怪政府破产了。

要了解希腊，我们必须去小岛。

希腊人说，在他们所有的岛屿中，总会有一个，你一定会爱上并回来。问题是，我能记住哪一个吗？

我们再次启航。

“这是爱琴海吗？”我无知地问道。

“好问题。”船长说，“这是地中海的一部分。我们喜欢称它为爱琴海。它更浪漫。你不这么认为吗？”

我们停留的第一个岛是提洛岛。

除了考古学家，没有人住在那里了。岛上到处都是商店、剧院和妓院的废墟，这些都是曾经繁荣的城市的遗迹。在公元前300年，它的污水系统比今天的一些第三世界国家先进得多。

在众多岛屿中，最受欢迎的是圣托里尼岛。小镇就在高高的悬崖上，上面覆盖着雪！随着船越来越近，我们意识到“雪”实际上是白色房屋，蓝色屋顶消失在蓝天中。

我们坐车到了山顶，看到了很多教堂。它们属于希腊东正教。最上面的那个有三排铃铛。第一排一个，第二排三个，第三排五个。与其爬上所有的台阶，不如选择骑驴上山。它们脖子上挂着一个写着“出租车”的徽章。

从顶部可以看到带有蓝色游泳池、餐厅和商店的别墅。还有一个风车，但只剩下骨架了。

然而最有特色的还是猫。我从来没有在其他地方见过这么多。每个人都给它们拍照。有无数关于这些猫的图画书。

我们回到船上喝“茴香酒”，这是当地最受欢迎的酒。配上新鲜的腰果、核桃、松子和开心果，任何饮料都会很好喝。

往往是你遇到的人比风光给你留下更深的印象。

我们在帕罗斯岛的导游不是当地人，而是来自德国。她一定已经五十多岁了，看起来有点像瓦妮萨·雷德格雷夫。几年前她来到这个岛上并留下来。她没有告诉我们历史和地理，而是指着一座教堂。“你看到不远处的教堂了吗？相传中间有一条隧道。我们不知道谁在挖掘中贡献最大。我肯定是修女们。”

“希腊有很多岛屿。为什么选择这个留下来？”我问她。

“我喜欢这里的传统，”她回答道。“人死后，尸体会被埋葬三年。然后挖出来，用酒洗干净。然后将其放在一个盒子里，与家人一起生活。”

她在没有电的家里请我们吃午饭。她用某种木材烧烤某些肉。

“我相信你能看出区别。”她说。

确实，我可以。

当她听说我是兼职作家时，她告诉我，我有一天会回到这个岛上。“山上的房子曾经是当地的一家旅馆。由于现在每个人都去美国大连锁店，没有更多的客人愿意留在那里。政府已经把它变成作家的住所。如果他们在这个岛上写一两篇文章，他们就可以免费入住。”

这让我爱上了帕罗斯，我必须回去写一本书。

印第安纳·琼斯的粉红大门

在去埃及之前，我摔断了腿。

我去过那里很多次了，没有什么可以探索的了。也许新博物馆建成后我会再去。

从那里我不得不再飞四个小时才能到达约旦首都安曼。当我们还是孩子的时候，在电影开始之前，电影院会放映一小段新闻纪录片。每当我们看到查尔斯王子模仿他的父亲，双手背在身后走路时，我们也会看到年轻的约旦国王，因为当时这个国家是英国的殖民地。现在，他们都是老人。

不过，约旦国王的工作比查尔斯王子更难。约旦没有石油。他不断受到来自伊拉克的威胁，必须与以色列保持友好关系。在他聪明的领导下，约旦人民成为中东的精英。

开车花了六个小时才到达佩特拉。腿断了，本来打算租一辆马车的，但弯弯曲曲的小路可能会把我扔出去，所以我选择了蹒跚前行。

步行实际上很容易，一路下坡，然后，砰！巨大的大门就在你面前，全是粉红色的！无论你在电影或纪录片中看过多少次，这种亲眼所见的震撼绝对不一样。

玫瑰门由艺术家雕刻而成，以赞美丰收。

离佩特拉不远就是著名的死海。一个人真的可以漂浮！适合腿部受伤的人！请注意不要让水碰到眼睛。它会让你痛得要命。

约旦是游客参观《圣经》遗址最安全的地方。我看到大部分游客都是美国人，他们都长得像伍迪·艾伦（Woody Allen）。

极光不是绿色的

我们想看北极光。还有什么地方比冰岛更好？

我的朋友廖先生有一架私人飞机。我们飞往乌鲁木齐。从那里到赫尔辛基加油，然后直接到冰岛首都雷克雅未克。

从飞机上往下看，一切都是白色的。雷克雅未克是一个小镇，到处都是五颜六色的小屋，看起来像用乐高积木建的。我们搬到了一家专门为看极光而建的木屋式酒店。每个人都带着他们昂贵的三脚架、长焦镜头、哈苏和徕卡。与这一切相比，我的iPhone手机看起来很不起眼。

最好的啤酒被称为Gull，食物没什么可写的，除了海雀肉，我以前没试过。后来我发现这也没什么好写的。

“今晚天气晴朗，”酒店经理说，“我们有一个很好的机会看到极光！”

“我认为我们不会那么幸运，”另一位客人说，“上次在芬兰我们等了三个晚上，连星星都没有！”他是对的，我们什么也没看到。

但在第二天晚上，奇迹确实发生了。

经理宣布：“光！光！光！”就像潜水艇艇长大喊：“潜！潜！潜！”

每个人都带着他们的装备冲进最冷的夜晚，兴奋得就像夏天一样。我们没有看到五颜六色的极光，而是一片片移动的白光。摄影师们都在抓拍，只有通过镜头，极光看起来才是绿色的。

但我们保持沉默。毕竟，我们一路来到这里，我们不能让其他人失望回家！

作家之幸

我在中学时开始写作。十五岁时，我的第一个故事在当地报纸上发表。稿费不多，但足以让我请我的同学去酒吧喝酒。只要你付账，没人关心你多大了。

多年后，我进入了电影行业，完全忘记了写作。

一天晚上，我和一群朋友共进晚餐时，我和他们说起我的旅行经历。故事很有趣，大家都笑了。

其中包括香港主要报纸《东方日报》的主编。

“你为什么不把故事写下来？”他说。

“我不能。我已经忘记怎么写了。”

“放屁！如果你能讲一个故事，你就可以写。把它写在纸上，仅此而已。别想技巧，只需要像你跟我们聊天那样简单地讲述你的故事。”他建议道。

这激发了我成为作家的职业生涯，我得强调，我很努力。我讲的故事很受欢迎，读者想看更多。有一段时间，我同时为两份报纸写了两个专栏，为周刊写了很多文章。

最终这些故事被编成了书。版税少得可怜，但谁在乎。无论如何，这些文章已经由报纸和杂志付过稿酬。

很多年过去了。

书籍的数量逐渐增加。所有这些都是由我的好朋友苏美璐画的插画。我们有三十多年的友谊，这可以说是一个奇迹。

一天在嘉禾影城，老板邹文怀走进我的办公室。他看到我在书架上的书，酸溜溜地说：“如果你出生在日本，本来可以赚到很多钱，你就不用再在电影行业工作了。”他说的话好像在批评我工作不专心。

“是的，”我回答，“但如果我出生在柬埔寨，我就会被送上刑场。”

真的吗？

我刚开始写作时，常收到读者的来信。不少人问：“你讲的故事是真的吗？”

记得小时候，我经常晚上到河边的一棵大松树旁。坐在那里的老人给周围的人讲故事。他划了一根火柴，不是抽烟，而是点一炷香。然后他开始讲述他的故事，从古到今，天南地北，引人入胜。

香火燃尽时，他瘦小的儿子会拿出一个碗，向听众收钱。有些人给了一分钱，有些人没有。他不在乎，而是继续讲述他的故事。我被迷住了，习惯在那里坐几个小时。

一天晚上，天色渐晚，他收拾行装，带着儿子离开了。

我走到他跟前，指出故事中的一些人物来自不同的朝代。老人抚摸着我的头说：“孩子，这些故事是真是假并不重要，重要的是，故事好不好听。”

那一摔

20世纪80年代是香港电影业的黄金时代。我们凭着成龙的电影成功征服了日本市场和世界其他地区，包括非洲大陆。

当老板邹文怀从他的办公室打电话给我时，我是嘉禾的制片经理。

“让成龙躲一下。我们得到消息，一个越南黑帮集团要绑架他拍电影。”

“去哪儿？”我问。

“任何地方，”他说，“现在就走！”

我一直很享受旅行的乐趣，我想到的第一个城市是巴塞罗那，毕加索（Picasso）、米罗（Miro）、达利（Dali）和高迪的故乡。

成龙、洪金宝、编剧陈健森和我，登上了午夜的航班飞往这座城市。我们住在维多利亚酒店的公寓里，我们可以在那里睡觉和自己做饭。正是在那里，我们从头开始构思了一个故事，并继续制作了1984年的电影《快餐车》，该片票房甚是成功。

从那时起，成龙爱上了在有异国情调的地方拍摄电影，我们的下一个项目是1986年的《龙兄虎弟》，我们在前南斯拉夫，现在的克罗地亚拍摄。

我从香港带来了一个由100名制作人员组成的团队，并开始拍摄。

当成龙不得不为他的前一部电影进行一次东京宣传之旅时，我们已经进行了三周的制作。他花了五天时间来回穿梭，没有任何休息。尽管如此，成龙还是精力充沛，一到南斯拉夫就开始拍摄。

该地点是一个废墟，距离萨格勒布约四十分钟车程。有两堵墙，中间有一棵树。成龙不得不从一堵墙上跳下来，做一个翻筋斗，抓住树枝然后摆动到另一堵墙上。这棵树大约有四十英尺高，下面的地面布满了岩石。问题是由于摄像机的角度，我们无法用纸盒覆盖地面以保证安全。

“你能做到吗？”我们问。

“小事！”成龙回答，“我从更高的地方跳过。”

当然，与必须从七层楼跳下的电影《A计划》相比，这算不了什么。

开始拍摄。成龙从一堵墙上跳下来，翻了个跟头，抓住了树枝，安全地落在了另一边。每个人都拍了拍手，但成龙并不满意。

“再来一个！”

（自从成龙出演1982年的电影《龙少爷》，这成了他的标志性短语。拍摄一个踢毽子的镜头，背后是2899次“NG（不好）！”。）

已经拍得更好，但成龙说还不够好。

“再来一个！”他命令道。

在第三次拍摄时，他从壁架跳到树上，但他抓住的树枝折断了，使他摔到地面上。

一声巨响传来，所有人都冲到现场。

成龙起初看起来很好，但当我们把他抱起来时，血开始像水龙头里的水一样从他的左耳里流出来。

我们试着用手捂住他的伤口。片场有一名急诊护士带着棉花跑来。

“怎么样？”成龙神志清醒，但声音虚弱。

“这只是耳朵上的一个伤口。”化妆师对他撒了谎。

“疼吗？疼吗？”经常出现在片场的成龙爸爸哭了起来。

成龙摇了摇头，更多的血流了出来，他开始失去知觉。

“别让他睡！他必须保持清醒！”有很多伤病经验的特技队喊道。

我们十个人抬着他穿过一条狭窄的道路，通向一辆等候的吉普车。前往当地医院的颠簸导致他的耳朵流血更多，棉签浸湿了。成龙爸爸一直亲吻着儿子。成龙全程神志清醒，只是声音变弱了，他说他想呕吐。

在我们到达医院之前，好像过了一辈子。但你还能称这建筑为医院吗？它是如此古老和破烂。

成龙被推进急诊室，在那里他注射了四针破伤风疫苗。但血流却无法停止。

“我们将不得不将他转移到专科医院。”医生宣布。

又一家破烂的医院。我们甚至发现天花板上溅满了黑色的血点。我问男护士怎么回事，他如实回答："哦，那是一个病人从自己喉咙里拔管子喷出来的。"

我反胃了。

经过漫长的等待，专家出现了。他是一个衣衫褴褛的家伙，一头乱糟糟的白发，抽着一根又一根的烟，一身白袍看起来脏兮兮的。他将成龙推入手术室进行X光检查。

在等待的过程中，我们设法给香港打电话，被告知我们必须尝试联系欧洲最好的神经科医生，但一直联系不上对方。

环顾四周，急诊室的医疗设备其实还挺先进的，和一般病房不一样。

一组四名医生聚集在一起讨论这个案子。

"病人的头骨有一个四英寸的裂缝。"其中一位医生用标准的英语说。

"他有生命危险吗？"我们都问。

"幸运的是，血液已经从他的耳朵里流出了。"医生说，"如果他的大脑一直在流血，他现在很可能已经昏迷。"

"然后呢？"我们问。

"他必须马上手术！"白发医生说道，"有一块骨头快要刺进脑子了，一定要取出来！"

听说成龙要在这家医院做手术，我们又开始担心了。

“如果我们现在不这样做，血液会在耳朵里凝固，病人就会聋，这是小事。如果那块骨头伤害了大脑，那就更糟了。”他又抖掉了香烟上的烟灰。

我们应该做什么？我们应该做什么？我们无法为成龙爸爸做决定。

就在这时，电话响了，是香港打来的国际电话。

“巴黎的外科医生建议你去看南斯拉夫最好的专家，一个叫佩特森医生的人，他应该会立即给成龙动手术。”

“但是佩特森医生在哪里？我们在哪里可以找到他？”

一直抽着烟，头发凌乱、灰白头发的医生笑着说：“我是佩特森医生。”

成龙爸爸在文件上签了字，佩特森医生安慰他说：“别担心，这和四肢的手术没什么区别。只是因为伤在头骨上听起来更危险。”他熄灭了香烟，把成龙推进了手术室。

几个小时过去了，另一队医生和护士在外面等着接手，他们也都是吸烟者。等候区像深山中烟雾弥漫！

佩特森医生出来了。我们冲向他，以为手术已经完成，但佩特森医生示意我们等一下。他拍了拍空口袋，又向护士要了一支烟。在回去做手术之前，用力地吸了一口。我的天！这会让所有老烟枪蒙羞！

又一个小时过去了，全部医生都出来了。

每个人都跳了起来，问：“怎么样？”

佩特森医生摇摇头，我们又跳了起来。

“我从没见过这样的病人！整个手术过程中，他的血压从未下降。简直是超人！”

“他没事吧？”我们喊道。

“是的，”他说，“但我们必须观察他一段时间，以确保不会出现其他问题。”

终于松一口气！

佩特森医生又开始吸烟。“在这里等着没用。病人必须休息。他十天就恢复了。”

第二天只有少数人被允许探望他，成龙一直昏睡。第三天，他开始抱怨头痛。医生让护士给他打止痛针，但成龙这辈子最讨厌打针。有八名护士轮流照顾他，但成龙只对其中之一感到满意。成龙说她是最用心打针的，但大家都知道她有成龙偏爱的高鼻子！

又过了几天，成龙开始讲笑话。

他说，比起插在他的阴茎和屁股上的两根管子来说，疼痛根本不算什么，这让任何动作都非常痛苦！

老朋友谭咏麟来看望他。他吹着《朋友》的主题曲，成龙跟着唱。

过了一段时间，护士们开始治疗他的伤口。她们试了好几次才把所有的缝线都拆了，但我们一直没弄清楚总共缝了多少针。

“你现在可以出院了。”佩特森医生终于宣布。

三周后，成龙又回到了跳墙场景。他做得很漂亮，但即便如此，他还是转向工作人员说：“再来一次。”

尾声

当成龙在他的旅馆房间里康复时，他问我是否要感谢八位护士对他的照料，晚上招待她们。我们与成龙爸爸和特技演员一起为所有女士安排了一顿丰盛的晚餐。

护士们悉心打扮后，跟穿着白袍的样子完全不同。盛宴之后，我们一起去了酒吧。

女士们点了Slivovitz，一种酒精含量非常高的当地烈酒。“一米！”她们对酒保说。一米？而不是一杯？我们以为我们听错了。不，不！酒保将Slivovitz装入特殊的小瓶子中，然后将它们排成一排，直到它们达到一米长。女士们拿起第一小瓶一饮而尽，然后是第二瓶、第三瓶和第四瓶，直到最后一瓶。一米又一米被护士们喝光。然后她们把我们拉到舞池，随着迪斯科音乐跳舞。我们不停地跳舞，直到特技演员和我精疲力竭。

直到清晨，舞池里只剩下成龙爸爸继续跳舞。

我们终于知道成龙的超人基因是从何而来的了。

布达佩斯吾爱

成龙被送往美国医院做康复，拍摄停止了。每个人都被送回家了。我留下来善后。

然后，我借此机会去东欧旅行。我一直梦想去波兰、罗马尼亚、捷克斯洛伐克和保加利亚等国家，这些地方都是德古拉伯爵传说中的发源地。从萨格勒布我去到了维也纳。有一条如此笔直的高速公路，连续行驶数小时而找不到任何弯道。

我晚上到达布达佩斯，立刻爱上了它。所有的纪念碑都被点亮了。昔日奥匈帝国想与巴黎抗衡，不惜重金打造这座城市。

第二天早上，安东·莫尔纳（Anton Molnar）来见我。他是我儿时的朋友Richard Wong介绍给我的。安东现在是巴黎的著名画家，但当时他还是一个苦苦挣扎的年轻艺术家。他坚持要我去看他的作品。我们去了一家意大利餐厅。墙上挂着一张年轻裸女的大照片，她的重要部位覆盖着番茄酱意大利面。

“这里的女老板要我拍宣传照，我要了十五公斤意大利面。这就是结果。”安东打趣道。

“聪明。”我回复。

“每当她问顾客想吃什么时，他们总是指着照片说，‘她！’。”

我笑了。照片中的那位女士很漂亮，看起来像中国人。

“她是谁？”

“她叫珍妮特。她的母亲是越南人，她的父亲是法国人。你要见她吗？”

“当然。”我说。

珍妮特的公寓在一栋古老的四层楼建筑中。没有电梯，我们只好爬楼梯。门开了，她出现了。

不化妆的她看起来更漂亮了。公寓里的一切都布置得井井有条。我看到桌子上有一个红苹果。它被小心地咬出白色的一圈。

她一个人吃饭也很优雅！书架上摆满了米兰·昆德拉（Milan Kundera）、毛姆、劳伦斯（Lawrence）、狄更斯（Dickens）等人的作品的匈牙利语译本。

当她去厨房泡茶时，我问安东我怎么能跟她沟通。

“她非常机智。她可以从你的表情和手势中理解。当然，如果她不喜欢这个主题，她就会装傻。”

珍妮特穿好衣服，我们出去吃晚饭。首先我们去安东家接他的妻子克里斯蒂娜。他和父母住在一栋两层楼的房子里。为了晚回家不打扰他们，他在外面单独建了一道楼梯。花园很大。安东说，在圣诞节他们会在雪下埋香槟。挖到酒的人必须将它们作为礼物保留。我见到了安东的父母。他们都和蔼可亲。克里斯蒂娜又高又漂亮。我非常喜欢安东的家人。在路上，我们经过一家葡萄酒商店，买了很多伏特加。我们直接用瓶子喝了。我在镇上最好的餐厅给他们买了晚餐。酒单上有无数的开胃酒，我们点了十个。我们把它们排成一排，一一喝完，就像南斯拉夫人喝Slivovitz一样。之后，我们点了几瓶著名的匈牙利红酒Bull's Blood。当你还年轻的时候，没有什么能阻止你。

“我想跳舞。我想跳舞！”珍妮特哭了。

我以为安东会带我们去一些迪斯科舞厅，但我们最终来到了一个像高中篮球场一样的大礼堂。

一个四人乐队为一群年轻人演奏摇滚乐。每个人都像疯了一样跳舞。珍妮特似乎认识所有的年轻人，很快就找到舞伴。安东和克里斯蒂娜也跳起舞来，我继续喝酒。

午夜时分，警察来了，阻止了一切。当时它还是一个共产主义国家，大多数西方风格的聚会都是被禁止的。

当人们继续跳舞时，扩音器被移到户外。

隔壁房子的窗户像星星一样一一亮起来。突然，音乐又停了。警察已经切断了电力供应。

一切都沉默了。然而没有人愿意离开。安东和克里斯蒂娜失望地站着。珍妮特没有这样，她从鼓手手中抓起木棒开始以华尔兹的节奏敲打一个空油罐。有人掏出口琴弹奏《蓝色多瑙河》。我慢慢走到克里斯蒂娜面前鞠躬。我们开始跳舞，其他人也开始跳舞。远处传来小提琴声，然后是喇叭声，所有的邻居都加入了进来。三人组变成了管弦乐队。华尔兹变成匈牙利狂想曲。

我们一直跳到早上。是时候告别了。

我们相互拥抱。

“当匈牙利人交朋友时，他们就交了一辈子的朋友。”安东说。

“中国人也是。”我附和道。

即使过了四十年，我们仍然保持联系。

爱猫人与猫情人

当猫用它们的大眼睛看着你时，你不知道它们在想什么。事实上，你不必知道。只需要爱它们。

当猫想和你一起玩时，它们会过来用身体摩擦你。你通过抚摸它们的背部来回应，然后逐渐移动你的手指来挠它们的下巴。它们会闭上眼睛，幸福地微笑。是的，你可以看到它们微笑。这对我们人类来说也是非常治愈的。

我弟弟喜欢猫。他曾经拥有过三十只。他养得起那么多，因为他和我父母住在新加坡一栋带大花园的两层楼房里。

那三十只猫是从哪里来的？一开始他买了一个非常昂贵的雄性波斯猫。他精明的妻子建议，如果他们再买一只雌性波斯猫，就可以繁殖小猫出售。原来，这只公猫有点“同性恋”，对女朋友没兴趣。雌性波斯猫发情时，就出去扑向附近所有的公猫。

于是混血小猫诞生了。

宠物店不想要它们，所以它们留下了。然后是第二代和第三代……最终它们变成了一个有三十只猫的家庭。所有的猫都来自同一个奶奶，但它们的性格不同。有些聪明，有些愚蠢。我哥哥记录了它们的行为，他爱它们所有猫。单是猫粮的费用就相当大，但他并不介意。

猫会用前爪挂在阳台的栏杆上，等他从办公室回家。一只猫这样做没什么特别的，但是如果有八只猫做同样的事情，那就是非常有趣的景象。

所有的猫都有一个共同点，它们喜欢干净。它们会整天用舌头挑剔地梳理自己的皮毛。如果你扔给它们一个像黄瓜一样的长物体，它们一定会跳到空中。如果它们突然闻到了某人的脚，它们会睁大眼睛，嘴巴成“O”形。所有的猫似乎都以同样的方式回应。我哥哥还注意到，如果“年轻的夫妇”聚在一起，年长者会给它们自己的领地，并寻找其他角落安顿下来。它们再也没有回到同一个地方。

不是每只猫都可爱。我不喜欢波斯猫，因为我觉得它们很丑。或许是因为它们的脸是扁平的，眉毛皱巴巴的，这让它们的表情自然而然地暴躁。

我喜欢圆脸、大脑袋的。它们看起来有点傻，永远快乐。我父亲从不关心猫，直到其中一只猫总是挤在他脚下，为他做了一个温暖的脚凳。

有一次在日本制作电视节目时，我遇到了一只睡在人行道中央的猫。不管你怎么摇它、推它、拉它，它都不会从沉睡中醒来。我的剧组拍摄它，并在网上发布了视频。它获得了300,000次点击！日本人称猫为Neko。“Ne”是睡眠，“ko”是孩子。

猫对睡眠的热爱或许可以解释为什么它们必须被驯化，因为不被驯化，它们就会在野外被吃掉而灭绝。被驯化也有不好。

人类对猫做的最残忍的事情就是阉割它们。看到它们手术后吐出舌头，露出深深的忧愁和孤独，真是太难过了。

“如果你这么喜欢猫，为什么不在家养一只呢？”我的朋友问我。

可惜我住在没有花园的公寓里。当我看到我朋友的猫尝试把它们的垃圾用沙子埋在水泥地上，我感到很难过。永远不要把猫养在公寓里。

但还有其他方法。我的好朋友兼绘画老师丁雄泉是一个从不养猫的爱猫人。每当邻居的猫来到他的公寓时，他都会用培根和火腿喂它们。所有的猫都厌倦了吃干猫粮。它们非常喜欢培根和火腿，所以它们每天都来看丁雄泉。丁雄泉会播放古典音乐，让猫睡在他的画上。午睡后，猫会回家。它们成了他的猫情人。

微博

我父亲告诉我，如果你想做一件事，那就把它做好。从那以后，这一直是我的人生格言。所以，几年前，当我的朋友卢健生教我如何使用微博，我每天都在努力地玩。

在旧中国，一个富裕的家庭会雇一个有学识的人给他们的孩子上私塾。现在我们没有那么幸运了，所以我为年轻男女扮演这个角色。在社交媒体上。我会回答年轻一代问我的问题。追随者，或者这里被称为粉丝的人数增加了，我现在已经有超过一千万人了。但并不是每个人都有礼貌。

我的好朋友倪匡有他自己的处理方式。

如果一个年轻人跳出来跟他说："我操你妈！"

他会回答："我很老了。我妈妈年纪更大了。她不会适合你。你很年轻。你妈妈是我的年纪。她很适合我。"

我没有这样的耐心。我懒得争论。

"你怎么能阻止他们？社交媒体是一种游戏。如果人们对你不满意，他们只会诅咒你。"我的朋友说。

只要有强大的意志，必定有路可走！

我从我的众多追随者中选择了一百个聪明而忠诚的人。我邀请他们做我的护法！

然后我设置了另一个账号。任何问题和意见必须经过我的护法，他们负责控制质量。人们想说什么就说什么，但任何粗言秽语都会被过滤掉。聪明的问题会传递到我的个人账号。然后我会回答他们。

我知道这并不能让每个人都高兴。但你必须遵守我的规则。我知道这个限制会失去一些追随者，所以我设计了一种让他们开心的方法。

农历新年前一个月，我会宣布开放评论，在此期间，我的粉丝可以进入我的个人账号发文，没有我的护法拦截。

在那段时间里，问题会蜂拥而至。几乎所有的问题都很有礼貌，我忽略了不好的问题。每个人都很开心。

一开始，问题很长，但我鼓励他们问更短的问题。

以下是一些问题：

Q：你感受到代沟了吗？

A：是的，我还年轻！

Q：如何避免父母唠叨？

A：听他们的。不要按照他们说的去做。

Q：你能读多少种语言？

A：十几个。只限点菜。

Q：你的血型是什么？

A：我喝了这么多白兰地，我觉得我的血型是 X.O.。

Q：在你这个年纪，失去什么最痛苦？

A：失去了天真。

Q：你的缺点是什么？

A：喝酒、抽烟、不运动。

Q：你有没有想过戒烟？

A：是的，我戒烟了。我抽雪茄。

Q：你对年轻人有什么建议？

A：叛逆。

Q：女人身体的哪个部位最吸引你？

A：大脑。

Q：对你影响最大的一句话是什么？

A：做，成功的机会是 50比50。不做，零。

Q：为什么还要赚钱？

A：我的消费能力大于我的赚钱能力。

Q：你会尝试每一种肉吗？

A：如果你试过，你有权利说你喜欢不喜欢它们。

Q：狗肉呢？

A：什么？你要我吃史努比？

作者与我

过去三十年，我一直是蔡先生的插画师，这真是一个奇迹。一个星期画一张，有时甚至更多，加上两百多本书的封面和其他额外的东西，总共要近两千张插图，也许这应该进入吉尼斯世界纪录。

然而，蔡先生和我完全不同。

他的职业生涯是多面的，我只做一件事：插画。他周游世界，而我住在一个只有一条单行道和一家商店的小社区。他喜欢世界各地的美食，我以卷心菜、鸡蛋和粉丝为生。

我早期为蔡先生画的一些插图是关于喝啤酒的乐趣和赞美雪茄的。我从不喝酒，我对烟草过敏。他花钱大方，我则每天仔细观察电表。

也许我们确实需要相信命运。

杂志定期更换插画师是很正常的，所以每次给蔡先生完成插画，我都当作是最后一次。

生活在20世纪90年代初期，当时还没有“数位化”，杂志的艺术总监住在我附近，会在下班时将文章放在我的信箱中。所以我认为我能得到这份工作是因为方便。然而有一天我在街上遇到了艺术总监，他告诉我，蔡先生在一个聚会上对他说，他觉得我“领悟”了他的作品。

那时候，我的插图都是在麻将纸上完成的。打麻将时，人们用这种纸铺在桌子上以减轻噪声，但我发现它便宜且表面适合作画。在生产部门必须找到一个足够大的扫描仪来扫描图片，这一定是有点头疼的。有一次，设计师保罗让我缩小插图的尺寸，我说“我做不到”。我可以看到他在电话里翻白眼：“为什么？把纸剪小一点。”我没理他，毕竟你不能限制一个艺术家的发挥！

后来我搬到了香港离岛之一的南丫岛。有了传真机，我再也不用亲自去取那些文章了。有一次，它远远超过了截止日期，并且我还没有收到这篇文章。我以为我被放弃了。一天后，设计师保罗打电话说这篇文章刚刚收到，需要我在两个小时内完成，因为杂志要在当晚印刷。他说：“蔡先生的父亲去世了。”

我抓起墨水和一张纸，去了出版社旁边的咖啡馆。我坐在那里画了我做过的最快的插画：穿黑色衣服，鞠躬的蔡先生。一种深深的悲伤涌上我的心头。我敢肯定，那幅插图上有我的泪水。

1996年，我去了英国。路途遥远，加上蔡先生日程繁忙，是时候告别周刊了。

但蔡澜不肯！他说他会提前写几篇文章，并以某种方式说服该杂志支付每周从英国到香港的快递服务。不仅如此，我还得到了小幅加薪！

在一些不眠之夜，我会听到传真的咔嗒声和嗡嗡声，是直接从蔡先生的办公桌上，或者任何他住的酒店传来的。文章旁边总是有一些问候的话。传真的标题是*Bo Bo Tea Ltd*，所以我们总是叫他Bobo，他并不介意。当我们度假时，传真仍然会通过意大利小村庄的一家小文具店发送给我，当我走过时，那位女士会从窗户向我挥手，并给我几码（英制长度单位）传真纸，惊叹我如何阅读这些扭曲的文字。我的图纸确实变小了，现在它们必须适合快递文件的信封。

我记得我们离开香港之前，蔡先生在陆羽茶室请我们吃了一顿点心。他给了我一个亲手雕刻着我中文名字的印章，还有他写的书法。他还对我丈夫说："我希望美璐在我的余生中为我作画。"我印象中，这是很少听到和很少说的承诺。

谢谢你，Bobo！①

苏美璐

① 蔡澜因他制作的暴暴茶而被苏美璐称为"Bobo"。

English Version

I Choose to Live Fun

THANK YOU, THIS PERIOD OF TIME

During the Cultural Revolution, a man walked past a pond and found some duckweed. He took some home and put them in a teacup with water. Every day he appreciated how the plant grew. His wife watched and the love she had for him flourished too.

There are always things we want to do but never have the time. Being in lockdown we have found ourselves having all the time in the world. Let's do all those things we wanted! If we let one day pass doing nothing then we lose the battle. If we can do something like the man with the duckweed, we win the war.

A little pickle will improve your appetite a long way! Cut the hearts of any vegetables into the size you prefer, rub them in salt and leave for a while. Dry them in paper towels and put them into a jar. Pour half jar of vinegar and half jar of boiled water (tap water contains micro bacteria which will spoil the vegetables). Add some sugar and turn the jar upside down. Leave it for a day or two and then your pickle is done. If you like your pickle savoury instead of sour, pour in some fish sauce. You can buy this in any Asian supermarket easily. Add garlic, chilli and a little sugar. It is so good you won't be able to stop eating it.

Make your own ice cream. You do not need an expensive ice cream machine, simply two sealable plastic bags. Ice cream is not difficult, it is just made from ice and cream! Put cream with condensed milk in a small sealable bag. Then put ice and lots of sea salt in a large bag. Place the small bag inside the big and shake vigorously. Ice cream has now been made. If in doubt, watch a video on YouTube.

Write down your resume and squeeze it into a QR code. Use it for your social media to save time telling people about yourself.

Compile a list of songs and music that you have liked in the past. Share it with others.

Write emails to your old friends. Send them photos you took together.

There are hundreds of things you have been wanting to learn. Study them now.

There are thousands of things you have been wanting to do but did not have the time. Do them now.

My accomplishment is this book in English, for my friends who do not read Chinese.

I hope you like it.

ITALIAN NAME

My name is Chua Lam in my native language Chiu Chow, and Cai Lan in Mandarin. It was difficult for my Spanish crew to remember. So, one day they gathered and said to me, "We have decided to call you Mario!"

"We are in Spain!" I protested. "Give me a Spanish name like Jose,

Leonardo or Javier instead! Why Italian?"

They answered in unison, "Because you eat like one!"

THE BIG TOY

The greatest joy of being a producer is to treat making a movie like a big toy.

When I first came to Hong Kong, traditional brothels were banned. I heard so many interesting stories about them from the older people I met. So I decided to produce a movie called "Profiles of Pleasure" about this period.

I chose a director who used to be a production designer and was meticulous about his work detail. He studied everything and built a set in the Golden Harvest studio with a certain rawness about the whole thing.

The twenty-course cuisine on the table was carefully researched and recreated, including bottles of antique Hennessy Brandy. The movie starred the most beautiful actresses and it was fun for me to design Cheongsam for the ladies.

For the role of the rich client, I decided to guest star my good friend Nee Kuang who was quite famous in Hong Kong, appearing in a variety of TV shows, newspapers and magazines.

When I saw everything was in place and that the shooting would take the whole night, I went home.

In the middle of the night, my phone rang.

"Mr. Nee drank up the four bottles of brandy and has completely passed out! What am I to do?" The director was in a panic.

"You mean to tell me you haven't seen any drunken man in bars before?" I answered coolly.

"I know what to do," the director said.

He shot the scene with all the girls laughing at an unconscious Mr. Nee.

KITCHEN HAZARD

In Barcelona, Jackie, Samo and I lived in apartments with individual kitchens. When we were not filming, we would cook and cook and cook.

One day, Samo ran out of chillies and asked his wife to borrow some from me.

I grabbed a bunch of Habaneros and handed them to her.

Without knowing that these were one of the hottest chillies in the world, Samo said disparagingly, "Chua Lam is a really stingy fellow giving me these dry old chillies."

He chopped up the Habaneros and the phone rang. Forgetting to wash his hands, he picked the receiver and had a chat with his friend. After he hung up, he went to the loo.

He was on fire for three days.

IRON CHEF EPISODE

The Iron Chef was the most extravagant Japanese cooking show in the nineties when the country's economy was booming. In one episode the cost of food alone could go as high as US$7,115,520. The TV show was so successful that it lasted nearly 7 years and continued to influence all the food shows in the world until this day.

All the best chefs in the world, including Alain Passard and Pierre Gagnaire were lured into competing with the Japanese Iron Chefs every week. The show invited me as the guest judge because of my knowledge of food. I said "yes", only if I could say what I want. The other judges were polite but not me. So the Japanese gave me a nickname, "Karakuchi" which means chilli mouth.

When the Best Iron Chef, Michiba Rokusaburo presented me with a dish of lobster, I said to him, "Take it away, it's too tough."

He bowed deeply and accepted the comment by replying, "Yes, I overcooked it."

The audience cheered, for they were getting tired of politeness and they loved me.

I was asked to return many times. During the show, I noticed the verdict was not always fair.

There were three judges, two of them were Japanese. They always sided with the TV station. They felt if their own Iron Chefs lost too often, they would lose face. So the two Japanese judges gave higher marks to the Iron Chefs to make sure they won instead of the challenger.

This annoyed me, so I cooked up a scheme to counter it.

The full mark was 10. The two Japanese judges, being polite in their nature, would give the Iron Chef 8 and the challenger 5 or 6. If the challenger was a better cook, I would give him 10 and the Iron Chef 0. It balanced the winning points in favour of the challenger whom I liked.

This happened a few times. The TV station got smart and increased the number of judges to four or even five. I lost interest and never appeared on the show again.

Well, the guest appearances as a judge opened doors for me to the best restaurants in Japan. Even Nobu treated me as a VIP when I walked into his TriBeCa restaurant. Years later, I retired from movie making and led groups of top gourmets to eat around the world. I managed to get reservations at the finest restaurants in Japan.

Another funny thing happened not too long ago. I received a big sum of money as royalties for image rights.

A Pachinko machine maker used content from the "Iron Chef" to create a game. They made it very difficult for the iron balls to enter the "Karakuchi" hole!

THE STATUE

Years ago, I produced a movie based on the Chinese classic novel "The Water Margin." One scene involved the hero fighting a tiger. We did our research and found a tiger in Thailand. It had acted in many Thai movies and had become quite a star. We arrived in the jungle with a temple up on the hill.

The children in the nearby villages gathered to marvel at it. The tiger seemed friendly.

"Does it like children?" I asked.

"Yes," the trainer replied humorously, "for food."

Everything was set and we were ready to begin filming.

Suddenly, dark clouds gathered and a strong wind started to blow. The camera jammed. The tiger went on strike. Everything went wrong.

We had to stop filming and I was in a panic. There was nothing I could do except run around in circles. The local production manager saw this and said to me, "This is the holy ground of a temple. Since you are working here, why not go to the temple and pray?"

As I could not do anything else, it sounded like a good idea. I climbed up the hill with offerings. The temple was one of the smallest I had seen. The Buddha statue was made of stone. The roof had been blown off and the statue was exposed to wind and rain. Its face was blurred and expressionless. Usually believers would cover the statue with gold leaf, but not this one. Business must have been bad. Nobody ever came here to pray.

I knelt down in front of the statue and began to bargain, "I am no Buddhist and I don't believe in God. I came here to ask for smooth filming. If there is a true God, please show me a sign in ten minutes, or else I will leave without wasting time."

Ten minutes passed. I seemed to be enlightened.

There were no miracles, but the impression of the statue settled in my mind.

I made a deep bow and returned to where I came from.

The director was yelling, the crew surrounded me and kept asking, "What shall we do? What shall we do?"

I did not say a thing. I just looked at them blankly and without expression like the statue.

Everybody calmed down. And then, a miracle did occur, good weather returned, the tiger began to behave, the camera rolled. We shot the scene without any problems.

Taking the hill road on the way back, we passed the temple. A ray of sunlight fell upon the Buddha, and he seemed to smile.

THE RUMOUR

It is true that Bruce Lee died in the apartment of the actress Ting Pei.

It is also true that his body was found in her bed. But other rumours were not confirmed. There is a story, seldom heard,which goes like this:

When the police arrived, a large group of reporters had gathered. They saw the body covered in a sheet being carried out. Everybody rushed in and shouted the same question, "Is it true that Bruce Lee died in the middle of having sex?"

The medic drove the ambulance away without giving any answer.

Of course, the reporters and photographers jumped into cars and taxis and followed. At the morgue, the body was swiftly wheeled in and the doors were closed.

Hours passed. They waited anxiously.

The door opened and a shabby character from the morgue came out for a smoke.

"Is it true that Bruce Lee's lower part was still left upstanding?" This was rumoured by everybody.

"It's true," came the answer.

"Ow!" Everyone was gripped.

"Please let us in to take a photo," they all begged.

"It will cost you," the shabby caretaker announced.

"How much? How much?" they all screamed at the same time.

"500 Dollars."

Five hundred in the early seventies was a large sum and they hesitated.

The caretaker turned to leave.

"Wait! Wait!" they shouted. "At least you have to let one of us take a look before we call for permission."

The caretaker scratched his head and nodded unwillingly.

One of the reporters was chosen. The caretaker opened up a small gap to let him peep.

And Lo! There was an object standing rock-firm under the bed sheet!

He returned and confirmed it to his colleagues.

There were no mobile phones then, so everybody lined up at the phone booth. With such big news, of course the editors said, "Yes!"

After all of them had handed over the money to the caretaker, he instructed, "All of you! Enter one by one! "

Everybody was trying to grasp the opportunity to take the first shot and in the chaos no one heard his words, they all rushed in together.

There was no time for the caretaker to stop them.

The door was thrown open wide, and in blew a strong gust of wind.

The sheet was blown up in the air.

There lay two pillows lined up vertically and a pair of chopsticks stuck in between.

There was no body and no erection.

Everybody wanted their money back, but the caretaker was nowhere to be found.

LEE VAN CLEEF'S HAIRPIECE

In the seventies, Shaw Brothers ventured out with lots of co-productions and I was involved in all of them.

The first was with Hammer Films, a British company specialising in horror movies. I had watched all their Dracula films since I was a kid and loved every one of them.

When I heard that my favourite actor Peter Cushing was coming to the studios to make "The Legend of the Seven Golden Vampires", I was thrilled.

Peter was tall and lean and a man of few words.

"Mr Cushing, are you always so serious?" I asked.

"Who would believe a smiling Vampire Killer?" he joked. "As an actor I have to get in the mood."

There were many other actors too. I remember Lee Van Cleef very well when he came here to make "Blood Money", a Kung Fu Spaghetti Western, alternately known as "The Stranger and the Gunfighter" in the States.

Lee was only forty-nine them, but already he looked quite old. He was bald in the middle of his head, leaving a rim of hair at the sides. He was never without a drink, one bottle of vodka after another. He was drunk all the time, even when he was filming.

He had a wig made specially for him. It was a round hairpiece that was the same length no matter which way you looked at it. When he was called on set, he just plastered the wig in the centre of his head. He looked at me and grinned, "Convenient, yeah?"

I had to agree.

THE LOHMANN ADVENTURE

In the seventies when disaster movies were in trend, Shaw Brothers jumped on the bandwagon by venturing into co-production with Hollywood.

First, the director was chosen. The pick was Ronald Neame who did "The Poseidon Adventure", the hugely successful movie which marked the beginning of the disaster era. Then the cast included Sean Connery and Natalie Wood in the lead, supported by Karl Malden, Trevor Howard and Henry Fonda. What could go wrong?

Well, the disaster movie ended in disaster in the box office. Nevertheless, we did enjoy making it. A part of the movie was shot in Hong Kong and I was in charge of the production.

Neame was a gentleman and did not speak much. The cinematographer, Paul Lohmann was talkative, and we became friends. I learned a lot from him about the use of lights. For example:

"When the weather is bad, and it starts to rain, shall we stop shooting?"

"No, no. We shoot close ups using lights."

"How do you make gloomy days into sunny days?"

"Line up nine big 10,000 kilowatt lights and shine them in the same direction, imitating the sun."

"How do you know it is time to light up?"

"When you are in the room and you see the fluorescent lamp is brighter than the sunlight."

We drank a lot when we were not shooting.

"Why are you so ill-tempered, Paul?"

"It's my son. He is a good boy but has become a drug addict. I am always angry at myself for not having spent enough time with him."

"Is there anything you can do for him?"

"Yes. I stay close to him whenever I can."

"Have you ever tried meditation? It's the Buddhist way of achieving a natural high."

I taught him a simple method. The next day, he told me that it worked for him, and he would do it with his son when he went back home.

I did not see Paul again. I hope everything has worked out.

A MONSTER CALLED MOVIE DIRECTOR

During my forty years in the movie business, I met many directors. All of them were monsters.

In the old days, the image of a director was a guy wearing sunglasses and a beret. He would be smoking big cigars all the time, with a megaphone at his side, and sitting in an armchair with the word "DIRECTOR" written on the back. Later he became a long-haired hippie wearing jeans, hardly an image of authority. But they all had one thing in common, they would do anything to get what they wanted; they would sacrifice anybody, including their mothers.

How does one become a director? Well, some by apprenticeship, some through film schools, and some by their skills learned in certain fields. When the Kung Fu movies were all the rage, stuntmen might have the chance to become directors. There was one such director from Taiwan. When the Japanese cinematographer called it a day because there was lack of colour temperature, the director was furious. The colour temperature has to do with the light source. A candle emits a warm, reddish light,the midday sun, a cool or blue light. The sky was still bright, and the stuntman/director did not understand why the cinematographer could not shoot. He thought it was some sort of problem with the lighting equipment. Turning to the production manager, he ordered, "Bring more colour temperature with you tomorrow!"

The old school directors would yell, "NG!" which meant "No Good", the moment they walked onto the studio set. To show his authority, the director would NG the actress on her performance even though her acting was good. On location, if the weather was bad, he would order the shooting to stop. However, even if the weather was good, he would stop shooting too. A young assistant asked innocently, "Why?"

"The clouds are not in the right position, you block head!"

Young directors would make an imaginary rectangular frame with both hands and yell, "Shoot from here!", the moment they walked onto the studio set. The old European way was to shoot everything in one take, a 'master shot'. From there you went into tighter and tighter shoots, numbering them 1,3,5,7,9. After you had finished from one side, you made a revised angle shooting from the opposite side and numbering them 2,4,6,8,10.

Being inexperienced, the young director would forget to shoot 3 or 8, and then everything would have to start all over again, to a chorus of "Fuck, Fuck, Fuck!" from his film crew.

There were some good things about the studio system though. We, the production heads, got to see the rushes before the directors. The rushes were the first prints from the negatives, shots from here and shots from there, and they did not have to be in order.

Veteran producers could see if the story was not properly told and would order the directors to shoot more.

For example: a villain is being chased by the police, he climbs a mountain to escape but slips, falling to his death. The rushes show:

1. Full shot of the villain climbing up.
2. Full shot of his fall with a dummy.
3. Close up of him dead.

We would ask the director to add one close-up of the villain foot stepping on a loose stone, then a close-up of him screaming, "AH...!" This way the scene came to life.

The problem with some directors of the new generation is that they rarely read. They get their images from other movies, which make them second hand. That is why you get tired of all these special effects films. Artistic movies might be boring, but they have their audience. If you decide to make them, you must understand their limits. One cannot hope to make an art film into a box office blockbuster. I always explained this to the directors, but they never listened.

When I was with Shaw Brothers, we made forty movies a year. As a hot-blooded young movie enthusiast then, I asked Run Run Shaw the boss, "If we make forty movies a year which all make money, can't we make one that's artistic but loses money?"

He answered smilingly, "If we make thirty-nine profitable films and one which is unprofitable, why not produce forty that all make money? "

"As a film producer, don't you have an artistic conscience?" The movie critics in Hong Kong asked me. I replied smilingly, "I do have a conscience. My conscience is to make money for the investors of the movie business."

MEETING TONY CURTIS

"Tony Curtis is in town. Want to meet up?"

My good friend Bob Liu , chief of Associated Press in Hong Kong called me.

"Sure!" I said, I had seen all his films.

A star is a star. He made a grand entrance to the restaurant wearing a short, tight jacket like a bullfighter. Fans recognised him immediately, they asked for his autograph, which he gladly obliged.

With his piercing blue eyes, he did not look seventy-nine.

Tony's hair was grey and cut short.

"I miss your old hair style," I said straight away, "I used to copy it."

"You're not the only one! I tried to copy it myself," Tony laughed.

"What brings you to Hong Kong?"

"After I retired from the movies, I started painting. I am on my way to

London to hold an exhibition. I thought I would stop by to have some suits made. They do it in 24 hours!"

I noticed Tony kept pulling his tight jacket to cover his growing tummy, but it was not polite to stare. I was also curious about his six wives, but that would be too personal.

"Can you please tell me about your experience working with Stanley Kubrick?"

"Ah! He is the greatest. He understands everything about the industry, including which theatre in which town is the best to show his movie in. The other directors would place the camera in the most eye-catching position, but not Stanley. He always put the camera in the most obscure corner to make the actor feel at ease."

"There was a scene in 'Spartacus' that was cut when the movie was shown." I said.

"Yes," he got excited talking about it. "I played a young slave serving my master played by Laurence Olivier. He was eating escargot when I rubbed his back. He turned round and looked at me and said, 'Some like escargots, some like oysters, I like them both.' This scene was considered very bold in the 1960s. Stanley dared to handle the subject of homosexuality then and he did it elegantly."

"How about Laurence Olivier? What kind of man was he?"

"First class actor, of course. Very calculated. Every move was carefully timed like clockwork. Not an interesting person to work with though." he said.

"Are you Italian?" I changed the subject.

"Everybody thinks so, but I am from Hungary."

"Have you gone back?"

"When it was still a communist country. There's nothing much to say about it."

"You served in the Second World War." I changed the conversation again.

"Yes," he was delighted that I knew about it. "I was in the navy in the submarine U.S.S. Proteus. Not very comfortable to be squeezed in tight corridors. So I quit."

"How can you quit in a war?"

"Maybe because of my good looks," he said jokingly. "They gave me an honourable discharge, ha ha!"

"How was life as a young actor in the beginning?"

"Oh, it was easy. Working under the studio system was like going to an office as Paul Newman once said. We worked, we lunched, we worked again, we dined and got drunk before we went to sleep."

"Do you still drink?"

"Not anymore. I don't eat red meat either. Mostly chicken."

But we did. Bob and I finished one dry martini after another. Tony was tempted and ordered a vodka for himself.

"If you die, you die," he said.

After a few drinks, Tony's desire for performance got stronger. He started to do magic with his fork, his cigarette, his napkin.

"This one was from 'Houdini'". The star still needed his audience.

"Every movie we made, the studio sent in top professionals to teach us. We learnt gunslinging, sword fighting and trapeze with Burt Lancaster."

"Did you learn anything with Marilyn Monroe in 'Some like it hot'?"

He knew what I was implying and answered naughtily, "Only saxophone, and not with her."

Looking at the yellow bag that I was carrying, Tony said, "You have asked me so many questions, now it's my turn to ask you one. Why this yellow bag? It looks like the one the monks carry."

"Exactly what it is." I told him. "When we were filming in Thailand, I asked a monk to bless us with good weather and he promised. The moment we started shooting, it rained and rained. The rain lasted seven days and seven nights. On the eighth day, I had to protest. The monk replied, 'But my son, the rain was for the farmers, not for the film crew.'"

"What did you say to the monk?" Tony asked.

"I only bowed. We became good friends. Later on, I found out that he liked cigars so I bought him lots. He gave me this monk's bag which I find light and handy. I have been using it ever since."

"I like your story," Tony laughed and gave me a hug.

"I like yours better."

ANOPHELIPHOBIA

The teachings of Buddha tell us not to take any life, but if there is any creature I could kill, I would kill mosquitoes. I HATE AND FEAR them, their extinction would not harm the environment and I really want them dead.

Being born in a tropical country, I have always been troubled by mosquitoes. As a kid I had to sleep under a mosquito net, but one or two of the insect were bound to get in. I got so used to them humming in my ears that I could slap them while still sleeping. Sometimes when I woke up, I saw a beehive of red dots on my arm or leg. I knew I had slept too close to the net.

Live and let die, taking blood from me might be excusable, but why leave me with such an unbearable itchy feeling?

Once when I travelled to Malaysia, while crossing a river, I saw a black cloud coming towards me, buzzing like thunder.

They were mosquitoes!

I escaped by rushing back into my car and rolling up the window. Too late! Hundreds of them followed me in. My face, my arms and legs were all bitten. I nearly died of itchiness.

I remember a real nightmare when I was shooting a film directed by John Woo in Thailand.

We built a house in the jungle to be blown up at the end of the scene. Everything was ready and we waited for night to fall. Immediately we switched on the lights, we saw white clouds of mosquitoes. In the back lighting we could see them clearly one by one. Their stomachs were transparent, they were hungry for blood!

Every one of them was a kamikaze. They did not fear death. They flew towards you and once they bit, they stuck to your body and would not fly away.

"Protect the actresses!" I yelled, for if not, their faces would be bitten beyond recognition, and shooting would have to stop.

All through the night we kept killing them with fans, fly swatters, magazines, anything we could lay our hands on, but they kept coming all night.

Dawn broke. The mosquitoes returned to their squad and so did we.

The nightmare continued, for we had to shoot another seven nights.

The next night, we came back fully armed with repellent, incense, coils, electric swatters and all the gadgets we could find.

"There is a red line on your face!" The actress screamed in horror.

In the mirror I saw it too. The line was straight as a railroad running down from my forehead to my cheek. A trickle of sweat had washed off the repellent and the mosquitoes had found their field of dreams.

When common mosquitoes bite, the itching lasts an hour or so. Not this bunch. They left the unbearable feeling forever. So itchy that you wanted to cut the swollen part open with a razor.

The night was long. I saw the local film crew disappear one by one. I found them hidden in dark corners with their eyes half open. There was a strong scent of marijuana. This was the only way to escape temporarily.

Another night passed.

To fight the battle passively, we got drunk.

I liked the local whiskey called Mekong. It came in small flat bottles so you could keep it in your back pocket. I drank one after another.

It worked. Not so many mosquitoes attacked me anymore. They really knew how to enjoy themselves. They only attacked the Hong Kong crew who drank Hennessy X.O. Brandy.

Another night. The monk who gave me the yellow bag came for a visit. I asked him how to get rid of the mosquitoes. He replied, "You make your living making movies. The mosquitoes make their living drinking blood. To get rid of them, get rid of the hatred first. Maybe it will help." It did not.

On the final night I had a dream. There was a mosquito as big as the alien in Ridley Scott's movie. I knew it was useless to get scared, so I said, "Howdy!"

The monster nodded.

"You must be tired of blood by now. Here, try this." I threw the monster a one-gallon box of ice cream.

It took a bite and I was sure that I saw it smile.

I gave it one gallon after another until its stomach was so full that it burst. Millions of little mosquitoes burst out!

I woke up.

Strangely, there were bodies of mosquitoes all over the floor.

THE BARBER SHOP

I fell in love with Korea during my school days in Japan. One holiday I took a boat from Kyushu and landed in Pusan.

From there I travelled by train to Seoul, stopping at every station for sightseeing.

In one small town, I felt I needed a haircut.

As I still had time before the train would leave, I went to a local barber shop. First, an old man cut my hair, then a young fellow washed it vigorously with all his might. Next, a young lady came along to give me a shave. She began by lathering my face and covering it with the hottest towel in the world! Then she stroked my beard gently with her soft fingers. Using a sharp razor, she carefully cut my beard one by one, while two young men massaged my legs. Finally, a facial specialist came to pick any pimples, before the other young lady returned once more to give me a really close shave.

Poop pooop! I heard the trains whistle!

I just stretched back on the barber's chair and told myself, "I will take the next one."

MY KISAENG

During my many visits to Korea, I became good friends with the film director Shin Sang Okk. He and I both studied in Japanese universities so we could speak this common language.

I treated him to all sorts of good Chinese food while he was in Hong Kong, and he reciprocated with Kisaeng parties when I was in Korea.

The Kisaeng are the Korean equivalent to the Japanese Geisha. They represent an art form for entertaining noble guests. The Kisaeng house was situated high up in the mountains shrouded in clouds like an old painting. In the winter, they burned pine branches to create an aroma fit for the Gods.

A long table was laid and filled with traditional dishes. Thirty for each guest, one hundred and fifty for five guests and so on. Fresh ginseng dipped in honey, tender beef stewed in soy sauce, mini hot pots, pork wrapped with marinated raw oysters, and countless others.

It was not possible to reach for the food yourself. All you had to do was to glance at your favourite dish and the Kisaeng would use a pair of silver chopsticks to transfer the delicacy to your mouth.

Each guest was paired with one Kisaeng. I looked at them and they were all as beautiful as flowers, except for mine who looked rather plain. I was wondering why, I was the guest of honour and was supposed to get the best.

My kisaeng gestured to me to drink up, so I did. She gave me an unsatisfied look and changed the wine cup to a bigger glass. We drank up, but the unsatisfied look remained. ①

Finally, she threw away the soup from a big bowl and filled it up, finishing it all in one gulp. After ten bowls of wine, she stood up and started to dance. The Kisaeng had a drum tied to her waist and started to beat it with two sticks. She spun round and round, beating the drum ferociously. Meanwhile attendants carried a wall of 12 drums into the hall. Then in a sudden movement she bent backwards to beat the 12 drums one by one on the wall. The beating became faster and faster with each spin until it reached a frenzied climax.

Everything stopped.

She threw herself into my arms.

The only movement was her chest heaving up and down.

Now I knew why Shin Sang Okk assigned her to me.

---

① It is customary for the Korean to drink up a cup of wine in one shot, refill the cup and pass it on to you to finish it. Then you return the cup back to him or her. Cup after cup passes back and forth and when you need a rest, another Kisaeng's cup is placed next to yours making them a pair. They are called "eyeglasses" and you will find everyone laughing at you.

THE HAN RIVER BOATMAN

A Korean Kisaeng never sleeps with guests, but if she fancies you it is a different story.

I was an exception because, I think, I treated this Kisaeng with tenderness and respect.

It was inevitable that Korean women had a lower social status than men, when they were outnumbered seven to one. Korean men could be very rough with their women. You would hear old jokes like, "My husband doesn't love me anymore for he hasn't beaten me lately."

The other joke was that before the Korean War, the men walked ten steps in front of the women, but after the war, the women walked ten steps in front of the men.

But of course, after the war there were land mines!

The Kisaeng and I had a wonderful time together and after dinner we often went to the River Han. There by the banks waited many boats. The boats were about three meters long with a flat bottom. We chose one and the boatman rowed the boat out.

He lit a candle and covered it with a paper cup. He whispered a few words to my lady friend and suddenly, he jumped into the river and swam ashore.

We had a few hours to ourselves, and after we dressed, the Kisaeng blew the candle out.

The boatman on the bank saw the signal and swam towards us.

These are fond memories that last a lifetime.

THE WIDOW

In my view, Korean women are the most beautiful women in Asia.

"But they have all had plastic surgery," my friends say.

Nonsense! When I first visited Korea, it was at the end of the Korean war. They were dressed in rags and had no money for food, let alone for facial surgery. "How can you judge that these ladies are the most beautiful?" you may ask by comparison of course!

You go to a shopping centre and visit the department stores. Over the course of an hour you make a count.

In Seoul you will meet about five women who are beautiful.

In Taipei three.

In Hong Kong one.

But in Tokyo, if you roamed the streets of Ginza for three hours you would be lucky to meet any.

Most of the Korean women are quite tall, with slender waists and long legs, quite different to women in other parts of Asia.

One distinctive characteristic of the Korean women is that they are honest and bold in expressing their feelings. When they love, they love wholeheartedly and when they make love, they yell out loudly. In those days, the walls of Korean hotel rooms were quite thin. You could hear the women shouting, "Yobo! Yobo!" which means, "Darling! Darling!" It could be quite embarrassing sometimes.

When I was producing a Kung Fu film that required a snowy scene, Shin Sung Okk, my good friend, lent me his filming crew. This was a film crew that had worked closely with Shin for many years. There were no roads and we had to climb the snowy mountains by foot. I had worked in many countries, but I had never met a film crew as hard working as those Koreans. The men carried heavy equipment and the women too.

Amongst them was a costume designer who was always kind to me. When we rested, she always managed to gave me hot tea. The Koreans like coffee and seldom drink tea, so I had no idea how she could find tea leaves and hot water deep in the mountains. She was about thirty years old and never complained about all the hard work but just smiled the whole way. I heard from the photographer that she was a widow. Her husband used to be the assistant director to Shin Sang Okk. After many years, Shin thought it was about time to let her husband direct a movie of his own. Given the opportunity, he worked hard but the film failed at the box office and so he committed suicide.

The widow never married again but continued to work for Shin.

Love affairs often happen between film crew members, but as the leader of the crew I would stay away from such things. I have a motto, "Don't shit where you eat!" Nonetheless the bond between the widow and me grew stronger every day.

When we were shooting the last scene near a stream, I heard the stunt co-ordinator shout for synthetic blood. Nobody could find it and then I remembered it had been left on the other side of the stream. Not to waste time, I waded across the stream and brought the blood to the stunt co-ordinator. On my return, I could feel nothing in my feet because of the icy water.

The widow, without thinking, opened her woollen blouse and tucked my frozen feet on her bare chest.

I was deeply touched.

After the filming was finished we did not see each other again, but we did exchange New Year's cards every year.

Years later, out of the blue I received a call from her.

"I am in Hong Kong."

"How are you?" I could hardly contain myself, "Are you still working for Mr. Shin?"

"I quit. I have opened a small fashion shop and I am here to buy goods," she answered. I put down the phone and rushed to her hotel.

She opened the door. Now that we were no longer colleagues, we had nothing to worry about. I checked the walls, they were thick.

Nobody could hear us.

NEE KUANG AND ALCOHOL, NEE KUANG AND RADIOS

One of my very best friends is Nee Kuang. He is the most prolific scenario writer in the Hong Kong film industry. All the Bruce Lee movies were written by him. He is also the best Si-fi novelist in China with five hundred best sellers.

I never tire of telling the interesting stories of his life, here are a few...

NEE KUANG AND ALCOHOL

Nee was a heavy drinker when he was young and became an alcoholic later in life. He drank at least two 750 ml bottles of brandy and 1.5 litres of Vodka every day.

Three preachers came to his house and told him how bad alcohol was.

"You must be aware of the first miracle that Jesus performed?" he replied, "God never told you not to drink. He just said you must drink with joy."

But one day, out of the blue, he did stop drinking. When his friends asked him why, he answered, "God told me to!"

"Please tell us in detail," we all said.

"I hate to be controlled by alcohol and have tried to quit drinking a number of times. People told me that it was harder to stop drinking than to stop taking drugs. One day I met a priest and I asked him, 'Is it true that if two people pray together God will hear us?'

"'Yes,' the priest answered, 'the Bible says so.'

"'Then pray with me,' I requested.

"So we prayed together.

"From the next day onwards, I never touched a drop!"

We all thought God had indeed performed a miracle.

"We have quotas in life," Nee said later.

"Maybe I used up mine in drinking."

His friends said, "but we saw you drinking with Chua Lam!"

"He is a connoisseur of wine! He only buys the best. My bad quotas may have been used up, but the good ones have only started!"

NEE KUANG AND RADIOS

Nee Kuang has many interests in life and he studied hard to become an expert in all of them.

There was a period when he collected shells. He collected so many that he had to rent an apartment just to display them! His thesis on seashells was recognised by the international academic circle of conchology!

He is also an expert on tropical fish.

He farmed thousands of them. He bought concentrated water from the Amazon, and then diluted it in the fish tanks to soothe the fish from homesickness.

He had many fish tanks made to order, huge six-foot cuboids and when his wife complained, he said, "They will make perfect coffins!"

Then there was another period in his life when he was interested in making furniture. He made cupboard after cupboard. Not sure if the finished products were perfect, he would lock his son into them and ask, "Can you see any light?"

Of course, his son yelled, "No! No!"

We admired his skills in mastering all these different things. Then one day when I was visiting, I observed there were six or seven radios on his desk.

He noticed my curiosity, "I like to listen to music when I write," he explained.

"Yes, but why so many?"

"Oh," he shrugged his shoulder and said, "I don't know how to change stations!"

KATO, THE MONK

Whenever I pass a monastery, I would think of him.

Kato was one of my best friends when I was studying in Japan.

There was a café we frequented in Shinjuku called Fugetsudo where many artists gathered.

One night an American hippie gave him half a joint. As he walked out, he was caught by the police, but he was subsequently released on bail.

Before the trial, he called on all his friends to donate money to him to hire a good lawyer. Not to defend him, but so he could to leave a proposition that marijuana was not as harmful as alcohol. He was prepared to go to jail. Now that medical marijuana has been legalised in many countries, this story seems ironic.

After I left Japan, my former secretary once wrote to me and said Kato had become a monk, and that one day he would come to visit me in Hong Kong. On one visit to Japan, I found out he was no longer living there but roaming the world.

Years later he appeared at the Golden Harvest studio wearing a yellow robe. I was so happy to see him again.

"Come on, let's go and have some vegetarian food." I said.

"No, if you don't mind, I'd rather you took me home and cooked me some dumplings. I miss them so much."

In our student days we were so poor that we didn't have meat for months. When I had some money, I would buy some cheap ground pork and make dumplings for friends.

"There is meat in dumplings," I reminded him.

"It's ok. I am not eating meat. I am eating memories," he replied.

After the meal, I showed him around Hong Kong and brought him to the premiere of my new movie.

There were many reporters from the entertainment media. Everyone was curious to know what on earth a monk was doing there.

Kato enjoyed taking photographs with the actresses and got very used to the flashing of the camera.

"It is called illusions and shadows in Buddhism," he laughed.

The next day he bid me goodbye.

"What will you be doing from now on?" I asked.

"I am going back to a temple in Massachusetts. I will try to build a pagoda there."

I never saw Kato again, but each New Year I receive goodwill Sutras from him.

He had indeed built a magnificent pagoda in Massachusetts.

GYUJIRO, ANOTHER MONK

I have another Japanese friend who was also a monk.

Gyujiro means "The Second Son of an Ox" and that was his pen name. I do not remember what his real name was. Besides running a temple in Oshima, a small island in Japan, he wrote stories for Japanese Manga and they were all best sellers.

I wanted to make a movie out of the stories he wrote, so I arranged to meet him at the Imperial Hotel in Ginza where I stayed. He arrived in his antique Mercedes Benz.

"The tempura restaurant in this hotel is quite good. Let's have some," he said.

"Aren't monks supposed to be vegetarian?" I asked.

"Not the good ones," he said jokingly. "They can marry too."

Gyujiro was skinny and was wearing a pair of round rim glasses. His hair was cut short and his teeth were stained with smoking.

"Are you really a monk?" I asked directly.

"Japanese monks are passed down from one generation to another. I was born into a family of them."

"Thanks for coming to see me in Tokyo," I said.

"Not at all, I have an office here."

"Office?"

"It's not really an office, more like a study where I write. It's also convenient for me to meet my girlfriends," he laughed.

That night we ate and talked until the restaurant closed. We had so many interests in common.

"Come and see me in my temple someday."

He bid me farewell.

I made a point of that.

Sometime later, I took a boat from Atami and arrived at his island.

Gyujiro's temple was situated on the top of a hill and was much bigger than I thought. Facing the sea, the scenery was beautiful.

Behind the temple was his residence. He led me straight to his wine cabinet and there were countless vintage bottles of alcohol. We started drinking to our heart's content.

"Running a temple is a dying business," he said, "that's why I have to write."

"You're very successful in whatever you do."

"Not enough for the way I live my life."

"I heard that people spend a lot of money on the ceremony for the dead."

Gyujiro sighed, "Not anymore. They would rather spend money on the living these days. And besides, the Japanese live longer and longer. There's little money to be made for a temple."

I didn't know how to console him.

"But," he cheered up, "I have invented a new business!"

He brought me to the back of his garden.

There I saw a very big incinerator. He patted it like his new toy.

"This is for burning the bodies of cats and dogs."

"So?"

Gyujiro spouted eloquently, "As you know, Atami with its hot springs is an ideal place for retired couples. Their sons and daughters seldom visit them. So they keep pets for company and become very attached to them. Animals have a shorter lifespan and when they die their owners want to do everything possible for them. That is when the idea of an incinerator hit me! The dead animal can be cremated here. The cost is 200,000 yen. If the owner wants me to say a prayer, it's another 200,000 yen. If you bury them in the temple and set up a tombstone, it's 1,000,000 yen. It has become a very profitable service and people have to line up for it. When the old folks spend, they spend more generously than their sons and daughters would have spent on them!"

I understood completely. One thing still puzzled me though.

"Cats and dogs are small. Why did you build such a big incinerator?"

He answered with a twinkle in his eye.

"Sometimes my wife nags too much."

Experience Life While Having Fun

PUT YOUR HEAD ON MY SHOULDER

When I was in secondary school, I was part of a gang of naughty boys who were always running away from class to see movies.

One of the boys was from a small town in Malaysia. His relative had bought a house in Singapore and let him take care of it. During holidays the bunch of us would have parties at the house and invite the girls we knew to dance all night.

Among them was a young lady with long, long hair. She was already working while we were still studying. At that age we all loved more mature girls and we kept on dancing with her.

The music changed from Rock'n Roll to slow tempo songs. "Put your head on my shoulder" by Paul Anka was the most popular song. We hugged.

Later My friend married this beautiful, long-haired woman. I was the best man and the driver. We drove to his small town. There was a lorry waiting. Inside it sat the local band. They played the theme music from "Bridge on the River Kwai" to welcome us. By the way, they played the same thing in funerals too!

It was the local tradition for the bride and groom to circle three times around town to announce they were married and so we did.

The wedding party was held at the school hall. Everybody was invited. The headmaster was asked to give a speech. It was not every day that he got a chance like this so he made sure it lasted an hour, and everyone fell asleep. I was drunk at the dinner party. The next morning, we parted.

It was not until ten years later that we saw each other again. I returned from abroad to see my friend. He now ran a petrol station along the highway. He told me that after they married his wife opened a beauty parlour. Business was good. After all she was from the big city and knew all the latest hair styles. But tragedy struck.

She got polio and was paralysed from the waist down.

"Hurry up! Bring me to see her!" I felt choked.

They lived in a dimly lit old Chinese house.

It hurt so much to see her hair messy and face very pale. The three of us held each other tight and cried. Calming down, she asked, "Do you remember how we made punch by mixing orange juice, lemon juice and a whole bottle of gin?"

"Do you remember you were so shy that I had to pull you up to dance with me?"

"Do you remember after we got drunk, we squeezed together under a big blanket naked?"

"Yes, Yes." I held back my tears.

The moon shone on the top of the coconut trees. My friend carried her on his back. The three of us walked down a small road in the village. We went there to see a bomoh, the equivalent of a sorcerer in Malay. She heard that he could perform miracles and insisted on giving it a try. I obliged.

We went into a bamboo hut. There were dozens of people sitting on the floor. All of them had brought gifts of fruits, silverware, clothes, chickens and eggs. The bomoh received them all without saying thanks.

An assistant lit some spiced wood. The room was filled with smoke. This made the atmosphere more eerie.

The bomoh started to perform his magic.

With a wave of his hand, a small explosion occurred. When he pulled back the mat on the floor, green gems and rubies appeared. Everybody was amazed.

All the people who had come for help gathered closer. The bomoh touched the head of a sick child. He was cured immediately. A man's swollen stomach flattened.

It was our turn. The bomoh took out an egg and rubbed it on the girl's leg. And then he cracked the egg in a bowl. Little red worms spilled out from the egg, swelling and writhing in the bowl. They were alive!

My friend and his wife bowed deeply and offered presents.

I knew those tricks when making movies.

The people surrounding the bomoh were obviously his gang. The little worms were compressed red paper hidden in his fingers.

When the paper came into contact with the liquid, it expanded to look like worms wriggling.

I did not have the heart to tell them the truth. How could I?

They were happy. They sang "Put your Head on my Shoulder" all the way back home.

I never saw them again.

A TOUCH OF COLOUR

Walasse Ting's paintings always fill me with happiness. The vibrant colours and joyful images, what's not to like? If I had just one touch of his colour, I would be happy.

I longed to make his acquaintance and one day when he held his exhibition in Hong Kong, Jimmy Lai the newspaper tycoon introduced us to each other. Walasse was tall and heavily built. Although he was in his sixties, he looked younger. He was surprised by my knowledge of his work and said he liked reading my articles and that we could become friends. I refused. I begged to become his student.

"I could never teach you how to paint," he said, "because I was never taught painting myself."

"Really?" I asked.

"Look at my work. All the lines are like a child's scrawl. It's the colours that captivate people."

"Then teach me how to use colour."

"Is it your ambition to become a famous painter? Because if it is, you're too late. It takes a whole lifetime just to have the chance to become an ordinary artist, let alone a good one. At your age you can only capture a glimpse."

"That's all I ask."

"Ok, then we can become friends."

"Friends then," I said finally.

From then on, I took every chance to meet up with him when he travelled to China or other parts of the Far East.

Once in Shanghai we went to a famous restaurant. Walasse ordered nearly every dish on the menu. "It's not every day that I can get good Chinese food in Amsterdam," he said.

The waiter came over and saw the whole table of food, "Only the two of you? Who did you invite that didn't show up?"

"Oh," Walasse said, "we invited Li Po, Picasso, Einstein and many others."

I made a point of going to Amsterdam where Walasse lived, whenever I could. I arrived early in the morning.

Jesse, Walasse's son met me in the airport.

Since then I have become a friend of the family too. Walasse had a son and a daughter Mia who lived in New York.

I booked the same room in the Hilton where Lennon and Yoko took those famous photos.

Walasse's house used to be an old secondary school. The wooden door was quite small, and he painted it with wildflowers. Jesse said the door had been stolen twice. When I entered, I found the largest studio any artist could ever dream of. It was a converted indoor basketball hall. The ceiling was three storeys high and lined with five hundred tubes of fluorescent lights so that Walasse could turn any gloomy weather into a summer holiday.

A strong scent of onions hit you. It was from hundreds of bulbs of Amaryllis. They seemed to be blooming all at the same time.

"Let's drink!" Walasse took out the vintage Cristal.

"Are we supposed to drink champagne in the morning?" I asked.

"Are we supposed to drink champagne at night?" he replied.

After finishing the first bottle he opened the second one.

"So," I said, "how do I begin to use brilliant colours like you do?"

"Don't learn from me. Learn from nature. Anything that is colourful is your teacher. Look at the kingfisher that just flew into the garden. Look closely. Can you see the colours of its feathers? Remember it, study it, recreate it."

"What material should I use?"

"I find acrylic is brighter. The best is a French product called Flashe. You can dissolve it like water colour or use it just like in oil painting."

He drew a woman's figure in black and white and said, "Go ahead, paint it in colour."

Recalling his many paintings, I splashed patches of colour onto it. He nodded. Bottles of champagne were consumed. Then the lessons went on and on until midnight. At that stage I was so drunk that I collapsed onto his couch and fell asleep.

The next day we went to the Albert Cuyp Market and bought tons of food. The most enjoyable one was the raw herring which we ate like the locals, head back and chew it. We returned to the studio to cook and paint and drink. They were the most memorable moments of my life.

"What material should I paint on?" I asked.

"Any," he answered, "paper, cloth, refrigerators. Anything that is monotonous and dull. Colour them. Bring them to life. Bring joy to them and yourself."

Which I did. I even painted my suitcases.

When I passed through customs people would recognise them. "Walasse Ting?" they asked with a smile.

Later I bought a thousand white neckties and painted them too. I don't mind if people called me a copycat. If I could inherit a touch of colour from Walasse Ting, it would make me happy for the rest of my life.

JESSE'S DOG

Walasse Ting had an American Jewish wife. After she died, their teenage son Jesse was so grief-stricken that he lost his will to live.

Walasse thought a trip to the Thai island of Koh Samui would ease his pain, but Jesse just sat watching the swimming pool all the time.

One day Jesse heard a strange moaning and went to look for the source. He found the ugliest of dogs, a real mongrel. Its body was covered in wounds and it was so thin you could see its bones. Jesse took pity on it and threw the dog the left-over bread from his breakfast. The dog swallowed it in one gulp. Jesse threw a tomato and the dog ate it too. In fact, it was so hungry that it ate anything.

From then on, the dog followed Jesse everywhere.The whole of Koh Samui island was filled with coconut trees and forests. The dog just walked behind Jesse silently.

When he was thirsty the dog would lick the morning dew from the leaves. It was forever searching for something to eat. Sometimes it would flip over a stone and eat the ants like a pangolin. Jesse found the dog had such a strong will to survive that it put him to shame.

One day the dog went missing and Jesse went searching for it everywhere.

The waiter from the hotel asked, "What are you looking for, young master?"

"Have you seen a dog anywhere?"

"The island is full of stray dogs. We use a net to catch them. I heard from my colleagues that we caught one just now."

"Where is the dog now?" Jesse asked anxiously.

"Usually they are brought to the police station to be put down by M16."

"It's all my fault," Jesse thought, "if I hadn't fed the dog, it wouldn't have got caught."

Rushing out of the hotel Jesse took a taxi to the police station.

"Ta, Ta, Ta, Ta!" a roar of bullets was heard. Too late! Too late! Jesse never felt so guilty in his life. He found many dogs in a pool of blood but none so ugly as the dog he loved.

He went back to the hotel and was sitting staring at the swimming pool when the dog reappeared by his side. Jesse hugged it immediately.

The hotel staff told Jesse later that someone saw the dog escape from the police van.

From then on, Jesse and his dog became inseparable.

"Papa, can I keep him?" Walasse saw the begging eyes of his son and the dog. He finally nodded.

It is a big hustle to bring an animal from Thailand to Holland. First, you must buy it an air ticket that costs more than a passenger. Then, you must obtain a health certificate from the vet, plus a bribe to predate it. For Jesse's dog, a special cage had to be made because the local airline had never had this experience before.

Bribery of the customs official was again a must. Walasse and his son returned to the vet, as according to Thai law, a strong sedative had to be given.

"You know there is a risk that the dog might not make it," the vet said. The decision was made, and the dog seemed to accept it too.

When the vet gave the injection, the dog did not resist.

Their troubles seemed endless. There was no direct flight to Amsterdam, and they had to change planes in Frankfurt.

When they landed there, the airline people could not find the dog.

"Maybe it has frozen to death in the high altitude," they said.

After a long search they found the dog had broken the cage and run off to the catering section where it had munched its way through the first-class meals and was now sleeping peacefully.

At this point Jesse refused to let go of the dog again. They got off at Frankfurt and hired a car driving them straight back to Amsterdam.

Jesse moved to a country house with high walls to prevent the dog from going out. He nursed the dog back to full health and it grew a lovely long coat of hair for winter. In fact, the dog was so well fed that it had to be put on a diet!

It was a rascal! Over the years Jesse's dog killed countless chickens and ducks from neighbouring households, plus two young goats.

From time to time the dog would face the east where its distant homeland was, and howl and howl and howl.

MY CALLIGRAPHY CLASSMATE

While Walasse Ting's life was full of brilliant colour, Master Fung Kong Hou's world was only black and white.

When I was forty years old, I saw my life drifting away and I knew I must do something about it.

The obvious solution was to pick up art as a hobby. When I was a kid my father would use a brush and do all kinds of calligraphy to amuse me. I had always wanted to be like him, but my work in movies kept me busy and I had forgotten all about it. But my father had planted a seed and it was time to let it flower.

So I went to the best calligrapher in Hong Kong, Master Fung, and asked him to teach me.

On the day of my first lesson his beloved son had died of pneumonia. I was wondering if I should wait for another day, but decided to knock on his door.

"Come in, come in," he said. "It's useless to mourn. I'd rather use my strength to teach you."

He took out a piece of paper and told me to write something, anything.

"But I don't know how to begin," I protested.

"Whatever comes to your mind."

I finally wrote, "Thank you for accepting me as your student."

"From your writing I know which old master's style is closest to yours. This master left many manuscripts. You can learn from him. I also learned from him when I was young. When we both learn from the same teacher, we are classmates."

With tears in my eyes I held his hand.

From then on, I practised calligraphy day and night with a frenzy.

THE SMILING PINKY

Pinky always smiled. If she were not so beautiful people would have said that she was simple. She was called Pinky because of her dewy skin and rosy red cheeks.

Like many old stories her mother gave birth to nine children and Pinky, who was the eldest, had to work to support the family. At seventeen, when asked, "What do you want to be?" She raised her hand and said, "I want to drink and dance." And so she did.

"Singapore Dance Hall "was the best cabaret in Taipei in the seventies. The manager there immediately saw the potential in Pinky. Not only was Pinky an excellent dancer, she could literally drink like a fish. Big glasses of neat brandy went bottoms up one after another, her cheeks were already pink anyway! The thing about her that amazed everybody was that she never got drunk.

"Drink up!" customers ordered.

Large glasses of brandy were poured and Pinky never said no. Drink after drink, the customers would be lying plastered under the table while Pinky just kept smiling. This made her the most profitable asset in the cabaret and her reputation travelled fast. All the rich boys in town crowded into the dance hall to marvel at this treasure. Each swore he could make Pinky drunk, but no one ever succeeded.

Among the suitors were two guys who came every night. One was the son of a famous artist, the other the son of a rich merchant. The former was thin and tall with a melancholy look. Pinky noticed that he had the long fingers of a pianist. The latter was fat and ate like a pig. He always came with business associates and made them pay for the bill. Well, you can guess which one Pinky preferred.

One night, tragedy occurred. A fight broke out between the two men, but the manager was able to deal with it and stopped the brawl.

However, when the artist's son came out of the cabaret, he was ambushed by the merchant's son and his gang who set upon him with samurai swords.

The artist's son tried to defend himself and three fingers were cut off. The police arrived and the gang ran away. The artist's son was rushed to the hospital. The fingers were sewn back on but there was no chance he could play the piano ever again.

Pinky quit her job and married him. They moved to live in Tokyo where the husband worked for a big company. They had two babies, and the kids grew up in no time.

The husband came home less and less, yet Pinky never complained.

One day Pinky declared, "I am going to work as a Mamasan." A Mamasan is the head hostess of a bar.

"You must think of my reputation!" the husband yelled at her.

Pinky did not argue, she smiled and did as she pleased anyway.

The bar she worked in was in Ginza. Only rich businessmen could afford to visit this place. Although Pinky was now thirty-four, her waistline was still twenty-four and she still drank like a fish. The husband eventually accepted the situation. "The Mamasan never sleeps with the customers anyway," he thought to himself.

One evening a Taiwanese man walked in.

The bar girls told him that they had a Mamasan who never got drunk.

He got curious and he called for her.

"Drink up." He ordered.

The girls were surprised to see the Mamasan got tipsy on only one drink, and they were even more surprised that she agreed to go to his hotel.

In the hotel room they ordered drink after drink until the businessman collapsed unconscious. Pinky put down the bottle, pulled the man up, placing his right arm in between two chairs. She climbed onto the side table and then jumped onto his arm. The man cried loudly but he was too drunk to move. She placed his arm at a different angle and did the same again to make sure the bone was completely shattered.

Then she left smiling.

You can guess who the man was.

THE VAMPIRE CONTESSA

What a good time we had in Barcelona in the seventies ! Jamón ibérico, angulas, and goose barnacles were all relatively unknown in the gourmet world then and the price was reasonable. We bought them by the kilo in the Mercat de la Boqueria after we visited the museums. We rented apartments next to the Sagrada Familia so we could study Gaudi whenever we were free.

Down to business. We were there shooting "Meals on Wheels". The script required a big castle for the final scene. After exploring numerous locations, we decided on one, but the owner of the castle, a Contessa, refused to lend it to us.

After endless negotiations, the Contessa finally agreed to see me.

“What kind of person is she?” I asked our Spanish location manager.

“Oh, she looks exactly like a vampire. You will know what I mean when you see her,” he answered.

That night I was invited to the castle to have dinner with her. I arrived at the gates full of anticipation. They swung open automatically and an eerie voice on the intercom commanded, “Come down to the end of the corridor!”

The walk towards the dining room seemed endless and I imagined two holes has been punched in my neck and blood was spurting out. I opened the heavy door to see a skinny old lady who looked exactly as the location manager described her. She extended her bony hand and I kissed it like a gentleman from the movies. She smiled. In my mind’s eye I could see the fangs!

An arrangement of cold platters was already laid out on the table.

“You must wonder why the castle is empty,” she said, “I try to avoid people now that the age of elegance has ended.”

A bottle of red wine was opened.

“Ow!” I cried, “Vintage Sierra Cantabria, Teso La Monja Toro!”

“Drink up,” she said, “I have hundreds of bottles in the cellar but no time to finish them.”

I sensed a sad undertone and said, “We all have to go sometime. All that matters is that we have lived a full life.” She nodded. After dinner she brought out an album of photos. I saw her when she was young, playing tennis in Wimbledon, posing at the pyramids, visiting the Great Wall of China and the canals of Venice.

The wine was sweet, and we laughed at each other’s stories.

"We don't look so horrible when we get to know each other, don't you agree?"

I nodded and bid her farewell. Permission to film was granted.

One morning while we were shooting, I met a beautiful young lady dressed in a tennis outfit at the castle. I could have sworn I had seen her somewhere before. She came towards me and said, "I have come to keep you company. Granny told me you are an interesting character."

THE REGURGITATOR

I grew up in an amusement park.

My father was the manager and we lived behind it. In the fifties, the amusement park was a huge open space with movie theatre, cabaret, opera stage and many shops. It only came alive at night when it was filled with people. During the day it was fairly empty.

I loved to roam around after school to watch fat wrestlers making false moves, magicians practising card tricks, Kung Fu apprentices fighting each other. I also enjoyed the Fujian troupes performing and made friends with the child opera singer.

There was an open-air stage for vagabond artists to show their amazing tricks.

One day an old man came with his teenage daughter. I remember clearly that he had a crisscross scar on his left cheek and his fingers were deformed.

He drank one glass of water, then he formed a narrow hole with his lips and blew a jet of water back into the glass. One, two, three, he repeated the act and blew water back into three glasses. We were captivated. Next, he picked up a large fish tank and drank up the whole tank of water, including the goldfish in it. We held our breath, waiting to see what would happen next. The old man made a deep roar in his throat and suddenly he regurgitated all the water back into the tank, with the goldfish still swimming. We all clapped our hands.

The father and daughter settled down in the park and performed every night. After each act, the daughter would collect pennies from the audience. She had rosy cheeks and her skin was white as snow. It is a sight we rarely see, in a tropical country.

As time went by, less and less people came to see his act.

The old man had a few more tricks up his sleeve. His next act was performed with fleas. His fleas could jump from one arm onto another at his command. He also made sophisticated mini carts, tanks and silver cannons on wheels for the fleas. They could pull things one hundred times their own weight. After the act ended the old man showed the audience his arms and how the fleas sucked his blood. He said, "I feed the fleas and the fleas feed me." Everybody cheered.

I heard from my father's colleague that the old man and his wife used to be the most famous flying trapeze duo in Shanghai. In one accident he fell, wounding his face and hands, and lost his wife. From then on, he had to wander around, forcing himself to do other acts.

I became good friends with the daughter Shia Shia. She used to come over to our place to borrow books. My dad was also a scholar and he collected a house full of books. Shia Shia always sang English songs and the one she liked most was "One Day When We Were Young". I remember one hot afternoon, while listening to her singing, my eyelids got heavy and I fell asleep in her arms, did not have a proper bathroom THEIR DORMITORY, so sometimes Shia Shia would come over and ask if she could use our shower. Once I accidentally saw her plump breasts through the cracks in the door. I blushed with embarrassment. I felt so ashamed of myself that I had to run three rounds in the amusement park.

People got tired of the flea act as well. The old man had to pull the last act out of his bag.

On the stage was a rectangular wooden box. The old man took out sixteen sharp swords and ordered his daughter, who was wearing a bikini, to go into the box. Then he pushed the swords into the box one by one. With each sword the audience yelled out loud, they were in awe. After all sixteen swords were inserted, the old man said the audience could pay a penny to see how the trick was done. Of course, I was the first one to rush up and see what had happened.

There I saw Shia Shia in a twisted position, avoiding the swords by the inch. A penny, just for a penny, you could see my Shia Shia's body!

"No! No!" I cried.

I saw in Shia Shia's eyes that she was crying too. She knew I was deeply hurt but she was helpless. I was so humiliated that I ran away, tears streaming from my eyes. I avoided seeing the old man and his daughter for days and then I had a fever and fell sick. By the time I recovered they were gone. Apparently, the audience did not find the act interesting. I never saw Shia Shia again.

Years later when I was living in Japan, I was walking down the street and heard someone calling my nickname.

I turned and saw the old man. I was so thrilled that I was speechless. I pulled him into a fancy restaurant and ordered all the food I could think of.

"How is Shia Shia?" I eagerly asked.

"Oh, she left me and ran off with some circus people," he answered.

I did not know how to comfort him.

Looking at the dishes he said, "I am so hungry."

"Eat up," I said.

"I can't."

"What do you mean you can't?"

"I am a rat in the laboratory."

"What do you mean you are a rat in the laboratory?"

The old man explained as we left: "A professor from a pharmaceutical company somehow saw my act of swallowing goldfish. He hired me to do experiments on how food is digested. Every morning I have to swallow two eggs, depending on the data they are collecting, I have to throw up and spit them out in one hour, two or three whatever. I just know that my stomach has to be empty all day. That's why I am so hungry."

"Fuck the Japanese!" I yelled.

"The Japanese feed me and I have to feed the Japanese," the old man mumbled as he disappeared into the crowd.

THE FISHMONGER

The Mongkok open market was shrouded in morning mist. An ideal image for a black and white photographic masterpiece.

Among the hawkers was a young fishmonger. It was a summer day's. He was naked from the waist up, showing all his muscles.

In front of him was a big bamboo basket filled with eels, each the size of a long cucumber, and alive and moving vigorously.

Eels are considered a delicacy by the Chinese and they are supposed to improve sexual ability.

The fishmonger tied rubber bands on his thumb to prevent the eels from slipping. With one grip he caught one and nailed the head onto the cutting board. Then, with a sharp knife he skilfully sliced off the skin and the bone. The eels were ready to be cooked. I bought a few kilos from him and paid.

"You are a kind man," he commented.

"Customers usually pay after I prepare the eels."

"It's all the same," I said.

"No. If you pay first, I might run away when the police come, then you will lose your money."

"You mean to say you operate without a licence?"

"Nobody here has any licence," he chuckled.

"Do the police come every day?"

"Every day, nine o'clock sharp, on the dot. We are all prepared to leave before they come and only return when they go away."

I laughed, "It's very British. In the Malay War against the communists, their Air Force dropped bombs on Monday, Wednesday and Friday. The communists hid and came out on Tuesday, Thursday and Saturday."

The fishmonger asked, "What happened on Sunday?"

"On Sunday, both sides rested."

We laughed together.

At this moment a woman appeared.

"May I choose some eels?"

"By all means,"the young man replied.

The woman was in her thirties and was wearing a tight Chinese dress showing her feminine body. She picked the eels one by one, touching and fondling, and her breath became heavy. The sun shone behind the youth, casting a silhouette of his muscles and sweat.

Without a word the young man dropped everything and gave all the eels to the neighbouring fishmonger. For a moment I thought the police had arrived early.

Then I saw the young man and the woman disappear in the crowd.

THE ETERNAL SCAM

Years ago, I met a detective who told me the story of Ying Ying.

Old Man Chang was a junior clerk in the Hong Kong Shanghai Bank. His work was monotonous and his life boring. One night, Old Man Chang went past Temple Street, a seedy part of the town, and saw in the bookstall a magazine cover featuring a nude photo of a Japanese porn star. She wore no makeup and had the face of an angel. Old Man Chang fell in love with her immediately. An idea was born.

The next day, he brought a camera and took three shots from the magazine. One of the face of the star, one of the upper body and one of the whole body. After that, he asked a friend to print two thousand coples of each shot. He finished off by renting many mail boxes at different post offices. It was not cheap but Old Man Chang was willing to invest. He then quit his job and worked diligently at home.

He bought magazines from America, England, Canada, and Australia and jotted down potential clients from the pen pal columns. Then he sent out letters, each with a photo of the porn star's face inside.

Dear John, Donald, Antony, the names were different, but the content was the same: "I am Ying Ying, I am 18 years old. I come from a family of eight brothers and sisters. Our parents old and sick. Being the eldest I must work as a waitress in a bar. The customers think me pretty and come every night. They offer to take me out. Being Chinese and having high moral values I refuse and preserve me integrity."

Chang wrote every letter neatly with a pen. Life became interesting for him. Some letters got sympathetic replies.

Chang continued to write: "My greatest wish is to go to America for further study. But alas, I even have to use me savings of thirty dollars visa application fee for me youngest sister's medical bills."

Thirty Hong Kong dollars was about 2 US dollars then. Everybody was willing to help. Chang thanked all of them with the utmost sincerity. Some letters asked if Ying Ying had received the payment and how her application was going.

"Do you want more money to apply for visas for other countries?"

Ying Ying replied, "How can I impose on you for more? You have done more than enough."

The next letter came with more money inside. Among the letters the most enthusiastic one came from a lawyer from Oklahoma. Let us call him

Jimmy.

"My dear Jimmy," Ying Ying wrote, "you are my saviour! I think of you day and night. I got all excited. And unconsciously my panties was wet. To a young girl, it's such a shameful thing for me to write to tell you this."

Of course, the same letter was sent to Joe, Adam, Louis, Joseph and many more. "P.S. can you send me a photo of yourself showing me your muscle?" Ying Ying wrote.

More money was sent to her, including the requested photos, and they asked Ying Ying for the same. "Dearest John, I did the boldest thing in my life. I asked my childhood girl friend to take this photo for me. Let's say it is to repay your kindness. Will you consider me cheap? I worried..."

A half-naked photo with tilted pink tip nipples was sent. Tons of letters together with greenbacks, filled the mailboxes. The lawyer Jimmy from Oklahoma alone sent hundreds, but most generous was the guy from Saudi who sent thousands. Jimmy wrote that if Ying Ying could send him some of her pubic hair, it would make him the happiest man in the world.

Old Man Chang sent his. The others demanded the same. When Chang ran out, he had to secretly snip some from his wife's armpits. In the Shanghainese barber shop, Chang carefully gathered up all the curly hair. Everybody thought him nuts, but he just giggled to himself.

At this point Chang made his killing. "To my dearest, pubic hair means nothing, I want to give myself to you." He sent off the full frontal nude.

Jimmy went crazy and sent her the airfare.Getting no reply, he wrote to say he was flying in to meet her. Of course there was no Ying Ying anywhere, but just a mailbox. Jimmy returned to the States and reported the case.

The local police would not take it seriously as it happened overseas, but Jimmy was persistent.

The case was finally handed to Interpol.My friend the detective was hired. He ascertained which post office Jimmy's letters had been sent to, and for weeks he watched and waited. Eventually, Old Man Chang came and opened the mailbox one day, and was caught by the detective. By that time, Chang had two million dollars in the bank.

When the judge listened to Chang's testimony, he could not help laughing.

Chang was acquitted because of lack of evidence.

The deception act became a classic scam. Swindlers all over the world copied this trick over and over again. It is still used even now, in the age of computers with emails.

THE LAMA

As the head of production in Shaw Brothers Studio in Hong Kong, my job included showing VIPs around.

Among them were Princess Grace Kelly and Prince Rainier Ⅲ of Monaco, Benny Hill, Danny Kaye with his same sex wife, who scolded him all the way etc.

One day I heard the PR cry, "The Lama is coming! The Lama is coming!"

"Which one?"I asked.

"There are many Lamas in Tibet. This one is the yellow robed Lama. Very powerful too. If he puts his hand on your head, you will be blessed for the rest of your life!" I could see the PR was very excited.

A large troop of limousines arrived. Everybody in the studio rushed towards the back seat and stuck their heads in hoping to be blessed.

I saw no one care about the monk in the front seat, so I opened the door for him.

It turned out that he was THE Lama and the fellow sitting in the back was the local monk.

The Lama was a fan of the Kung Fu movies. I staged a fighting scene specially for him and he enjoyed the whole show.

I asked him what kind of vegetarian food he liked for lunch, he answered, "The Buddha never said we should stay away from meat. He did say you should eat whatever was given to you."

Lesson learnt.

"Are monks allowed to drink alcohol?"

"When I was your age I drank like a fish."

"And have sex?" getting bolder, I asked.

He answered peacefully, "there are many schools in Buddhism. In our state of higher understanding there are no limitations in life. But one should never, never harm another living thing, human beings or ants."

"How about marijuana?"

"Some of the Tibetans use it to get closer to God. I am against overusing it."

"How about abortion?"

"Life and death are arranged by God. If a situation forces you into it with no other choice, you are forgiven."

I bowed deeply.

"You have asked so many questions, it's my turn to ask you," the Lama said. "Are you a Buddhist?"

"No," I replied humbly. "One day I wish to become one."

The Lama smiled and put his hand on my head.

A DRUNKEN BREAKFAST

My mother was a heavy drinker. She drank brandy morning, noon and night. When Nee Kuang my good friend visited us in Singapore, we bought him breakfast. I ordered a table full of local delicacies. My mother pulled out a big bottle of brandy from nowhere and told Nee Kuang to "Drink up!"

Nee said politely, "But it's a sin to drink in the morning."

My mother replied coolly, "Son, it's nighttime in Paris." The concept of time is fun to play with.

Here is another story from the Tsukiji fish market in Tokyo. The freshest and the cheapest fish could be found in the small restaurants in the early morning. This was where the fishmongers gathered after a whole night's work. Once I met one man who was drinking heavily and I asked, "Old man, why do you drink so early in the morning?"

To which he replied, "Young man, why do you drink at night?"

You see, it is not unusual to have lobster at noon or night, but if you eat it in the morning, it becomes the greatest indulgence. On Sunday mornings I always visit the fish market and buy a big lobster for breakfast. First, you lay the lobster out on the cutting board, them pour some white vinegar into a bowl and dip your left-hand fingers into it. That way you can grab the lobster firmly without slipping. Using a sharp knife, chop off the head and cut it into half. Put the head into burning charcoal, sprinkle it with salt and let it grill slowly.

Next, turn the lobster over. Using a pair of scissors, cut down both sides of the soft underbelly to take the tail out. Give the tail flesh a few light cuts vertically and then cut them across into thin slices. Throw them into a big bowl of iced water, and watch the lobster meat curling up like a flower. Line up the flowers one by one on a plate, chop small pieces of red chilli and green parsley, and place them in the centre like flower stamens. Dip the flowers into soy sauce and wasabi and enjoy them like sashimi.

Meantime, boil the legs and shell to create a soup to which you can add tofu, lettuce and anything vegetable you fancy.

When you can smell the aroma of the grilled lobster's head, you may pick its brains!

Finally, open a bottle of champagne and play some Mozart.

A perfect breakfast.

DUELLING WITH THE SUSHI CHEF

Let's face it, it's nearly impossible to fully understand how to eat sushi if you are not Japanese. Communication with the chef is the only way to appreciate sushi. That is why the gourmet insists on sitting at the counter to converse with the chefs, yet this is quite impossible if you don't speak their language. It also explains why The Michelin Guide have awarded so many stars to the Tokyo restaurants. Not because the judges know how to appreciate the food, but because more sushi chefs speak English.

"WOW, wow!" and "wow!" they cried after the chefs explained the origins of the food and the years taken to prepare them.

Having lived in Japan for eight years and continuing to travel there every year since, I learned a few tricks of how to duel with sushi chefs when you walk into a sushi shop for the first time.

The fate of the customer depends on the chef, for there are no prices on the menu. In fact, there are no menus at all. When you ask for the bill, the chef uses his sharp knife and makes a few strokes on the cutting board. There are no fixed sums. The price he quotes depends on his mood. If he is happy, he makes light cuts, and when he is not, he cuts it like somebody who is killing his enemy and the sum becomes astronomical.

Of course, you can say I have all the money in the world and don't give a damn, but then you won't get the best cut, or respect. We must treat the sushi shop like a battle ground and the chef like an opponent in a duel.

"Irasshaimase!" the chef will yell at you the moment you enter. It sounds more like a challenge than a welcome. To counter this, you nod lightly and say, "Um" as if he doesn't exist.

Then you throw the first punch by ordering.

"Sake!" you command.

"Atsukan desuka? Hiyazake desuka?", which means "Hot or Cold?" he fights back.

At this instance you must give him another heavy punch by answering, "Nurukan". That means warmed or room temperature in Japanese. By the way, all the best sake should be consumed this way whether it is summer or winter.

The chef nods silently, sensing that you are not an easy opponent.

You mustn't let him rest. Looking at the big piece of egg roll, you order,

"Tsumami", which means without rice.

If you forget this word you just point and say, "No rice." Rice is rice in Japanese too. He will understand. There are only two ways to order sushi: Tsumami or Nigiri. The latter means with rice.

The reason for ordering egg rolls is to test the skill of the sushi master. Egg rolls are the most difficult to perfect.

It is done by beating eggs and frying them in a rectangular pan one layer after another. In between layers some masters put cooked shrimps and others put eel. Sugar and salt may be added. Too sweet or too savoury will kill the taste. There can only be two reactions from your opponent. One is that he knows you know how to appreciate his food, but more likely he will be thinking, "Fuck you! Who are you to show off here?"

If you see your opponent is expressionless you must continue the fight by only biting one third of the egg roll and staying expressionless too. This way he doesn't know whether you like it or not.

If you like the expensive Uni (the sea urchin) or Awabi (the abalone), your next move is to order Maguro (the lean part of a tuna), not Toro (the fatty part of a tuna). The real gourmet always appreciates this lean part of tuna. The Hon-Maguro tuna caught in the Japanese Sea is so sweet and full of favour that it is ten times tastier than the imported Maguro.

The unconvinced chef would think he has caught you out by giving you the imported Maguro. You chew a little, then you put it down and you order Gari (pickled ginger). Gari is a jargon between sushi masters and is often used to clear your palatte.

Now the chef knows what he is facing. At this precise moment you must throw out double punches by ordering Geso, which is the cooked tentacles of squid, Odori, which means dancing in Japanese, for describing live prawns, and Awabi no Wata, which is the intestine of abalone.

The chef has never thought this could be coming, While he has no time to defend himself, you make your kill by ordering Tamari, which is the soy sauce at the bottom of the jar, or Murasaki, which describes the purple colour, but never Shoyu which is the common name. You dip the raw fish in soy sauce and then add a little Wasabi (green mustard) on top before eating it. You must never, never mix Wasabi in your soy sauce because this will make it muddy.

You can mention casually that in the famous author Tanizaki Junichiro's essay "In Praise of Shadows", he writes about how beautiful dark materials are and that they should never be mixed.

At this point you buy the chef a bottle of their most expensive sake and finish the two thirds of the egg roll to show your appreciation. And finally, you call out, "O-iso", the sushi term for the bill.

The chef will bow to you with respect, and you walk out paying less.

MIXING TASTES AND INGREDIENTS

I love Shanghainese cooking. They mix savoury, sweet and oily flavours.

"Oily I can understand", my friend said, "but savoury is savoury, sweet is sweet, how can it be savoury and sweet at the same time?"

For people who have not tried Shanghainese cooking it is difficult for them to appreciate.

Once you acquire a taste for it, you will never tire of it.

Not only is it savoury and sweet, but they also mix pork and squid in their signature dish of braised pork belly.

"Pork is pork, squid is squid, how can you mix meat and seafood?" Again, my friend was wrong. You will discover that this combination is quite perfect.

To prove my point, one of the most delicious Australian dishes is the Carpetbagger. It is made by cutting a pocket on the long side of a thick piece of steak. Then lots of raw oysters are inserted into it before grilling. The taste is out of this world!

Applying this theory, the famous David Chang made a signature dish in his restaurant Momofuku. He used sides of braised pig's knuckle, raw garlic, chilli sauce, miso and kimchi, before wrapping them with sesame leaves. Of course he put in lots of raw oysters.

Foie gras is often cooked with sweet jam.

The Chinese character for umami is 鲜, which is made up of fish on the left and lamb on the right. Obviously our ancestors knew a thing or two! Go ahead and invent your own dishes mixing tastes and ingredients. It is fun.

AN OEUF IS ENOUGH

I met Paul Bocuse several times before he passed away. On one occasion when I was shooting a TV travel program me, I met him again in his kitchen in Lyon. "Can you cook something for me?" I asked.

"But I have not cooked myself for a long time," he said.

"I am not asking for anything fancy. Just something you do every day," I requested.

"OK, for old times sake, what do you want me to do?"

From my pocket I took something out.

"An egg." I said.

He scratched his head but obliged. He took out a porcelain plate and put some oil on it. Using an iron clamp, he put the plate on the stove. Then he cracked one egg in it. Rotating the plate on the fire, he watched the egg cook to his liking.

Next, he took the plate out and put it on the table.

"Voila!" He said, finishing off the performance with a sprinkle of salt.

"Each to their own when cooking an egg. This is the way to perfection."

From then on, while shooting numerous food programmes, I would ask the chefs I met to do the same thing. One day I might compile their "stunt" into a book.

Asked to cook one myself: I use a frying pan and put lard in it. When I see smoke coming out from the lard, I beat the egg and pour it in.

Immediately I take the pan away. As I scramble it, the remaining heat will set the egg. Only a few drops of fish sauce are needed to complete it, nothing else.

This is my one egg.

DOCTEUR CHEF

If you meet a French person and he or she asks you, "Where do you eat in France?" and you answer Paris, they will turn their nose up. If you answer Provence they will say, "But of course." But if you answer Perigord, they will take their hats off.

This trip was to visit an old friend Docteur Louis Muzac.

Perigord is four hours by train from Paris. The journey was comfortable.

Dr. Muzac brought us to his friend's restaurant by the river. It overlooked a broken bridge and an old castle. A simple line of big white paper lanterns was the only decoration producing a fairy tale ambience. If you propose to your girlfriend in this atmosphere, she would say yes.

The owner, a middle-aged man called Daniel Chambon, appeared and said, "I don't believe in Michelin stars. I am not a chef. I am a simple cook."

Black truffle and mashed potato. The flesh from frog legs was pushed to one end, making the shape of a small umbrella, then seared in butter. You can hold the tiny bone up like a toothpick.

There were countless delicacies which l fail to remember.

"Of course, everything depends on the fresh local produce," Daniel said, revealing his secret of simple cooking.

The next morning, we went to Dr. Muzac's cottage for a lesson in preparing Foie gras.

Before it became well known to the world, Foie gras was only a traditional food made by ordinary housewives. They made it at home and sold it in the market to make a few francs for themselves. Dr. Muzac organised the housewives in Perigord and made Foie gras production into an industry. The country folks thank him by supplying him with their best Produce.

"First, we must learn how to dissect it," he said, like a true docteur, of course.

He took out big fat pieces of Foie gras, at least three kilos in weight, and put them on the old wooden table. Then he used his surgical knife to take out the veins one by one.

"If the veins are not removed properly, the Foie gras will be tough. It would not be as smooth as silk like a true Foie gras should be," he said.

Slicing the Foie gras into palm size pieces, he put them into a pan and heated the lard. He chopped up some red shallots and fried them until they were slightly caramelised. Then he sautéed the Foie gras with cherry jam, red wine and rice vinegar.

Next, he took out a big blind pastry crust and lined it with pieces of Foie gras and the caramelised shallots. Then he layered slices of fresh black truffles on top. This process was repeated layer on layer until it reached the top and finally it was covered by a piece of rolled out pastry. This big pie was put into the oven.

"Who taught you this method?" I asked.

"My great-grandfather taught my grandfather. My grandfather taught my father and he taught me. We are four generations of surgeons."

The pie was ready. We gathered around the old wooden table to enjoy it.

I must say it was the best pie I had ever eaten in my life.

Looking at the table, Dr. Muzac reminisced, "During the Second World War, I operated on soldiers on this table."

THE KANPEKI ARAGAWA

In 2006 Forbes chose three of the most expensive restaurants in the world: Alain Ducasse Au Plaza Athénée in Paris, Restaurant Gordon Ramsay in London, and the top was Aragawa in Tokyo.

The best wagyu comes from Kobe. Kobe is a big city with no farms, so where does the beef come from? Each year they have a competition. All the cows from the neighbouring farms join in. Time and again "The Champion" comes from the Sanda area, thus the name Sanda Gyu.

Each calf is given a birth certificate, stating its father and mother, and complete with a nose print. The nose print is like the fingerprint, every cow is different. Aragawa served only the best of Sanda.

The restaurant only houses twenty-two guests. It was opened in 1967. There are no fancy decorations, except for the open kitchen which is equipped with a gigantic Bizen charcoal stove. The griller was there from the beginning of the restaurant.

There are no menus. We were served with the hors d'oeuvres. Choices were wild salmon, big fat eel, the freshest shrimp cocktail or lightly grilled abalone. Salad was tossed with sea urchin.

Now, how do you want your steak cooked?

Normally one can order rare, medium or well done.

This restaurant provides you with ten grilling choices:

1. Blue.
2. Rare.
3. Medium Rare Rare.
4. Medium Rare.
5. Medium Medium Rare.
6. Medium.
7. The one between Medium and Medium Well Done.
8. Medium Well Done.

9. The one between Medium Well Done and Well Done.

10. Well Done.

If you go with a group, I suggest that you order a few kinds of grilling to share. This way you can enjoy and compare their delicate flavours.

For "Blue," you can cut like slicing butter with a warm knife. To perfectly grill a "blue" steak, the outer layer is seared to seal the juices inside. No trace of blood can be found. Amazing.

What is the difference between Sirloin and Tenderloin? The former has a round piece of fat meat on the tip. I love it.

Aragawa houses the longest wine list. Every sip of Romanee Conti is different from the previous. It is good to go with the Sanda.

When the manager came to ask for my comment, I said "Kanpeki", the Japanese word for perfection.

KUROSAWA RESTAURANTS

If you like Japanese movies and Japanese beef, but you don't want to pay the Arakawa prices, I would suggest Kurosawa's.

It is run by his family.

In a two-storey wooden house in Tsukiji where the old fish market used to be, you will find it in a small alley. The building was once an Okiya, a place where Geishas lived.

When you enter you can see a big painting by Kurosawa himself. The menu is designed and printed like a movie script.

On the walls hang photos of all the films Kurosawa had directed.

Lovers of his movies can go through them one by one.

The cooking is done just the way he liked it.

A set dinner would cost about US $180 which includes hors d'oeuvres like lobster or abalone. Then soup of oysters followed by a main course of a thick wagyu steak done in teppanyaki, finishing off with Japanese melon.

As the steak is cooked in front of you, the chef will prepare it according to your liking, you just have to ask. There are no exhibitions of cheap tricks, just good old style grilling. If you are still hungry, the chef will fry up lots of big fat garlic cloves cooked with rice. It is a meal to remember.

Another of Kurosawa's restaurants, located near the Diet Building in Tokyo, serves Japanese noodles. The Japanese go to noodle houses not for the noodles but the sake. Various blends of them can be found there. You can also have Shabu Shabu, a kind of thin sliced beef boiled in soup, and other kinds of Japanese cuisine at a reasonable price. Give it a try.

You might even see Kurozawa in the form of a samurai ghost there.

LARD

I yearn for lard and soy sauce rice so much that I had to open my own restaurant in Hong Kong. My mum cooked with lard all the time and I grew up eating it! To make lard, she used a big chunk of belly pork, cut it into one-inch squares and fried it in a pan. The oil oozed out from the LARD fat, leaving crispy scratchings to be shared by her children. We could never wait for them to cool down because they smelled so good. We chewed them until our tongues were burnt and our throats hurt. After the war we were all poor, a bowl of rice covered with lard and soy sauce was the utmost delicacy.

Things change. Everybody uses vegetable oil now because lard is labelled "UNHEALTHY". It has become the daily evil in our lives. No restaurant dares to use it. The cooking is less and less tasty, but nobody complains.

When we went to a French restaurant, they gave us bread and butter. Since it took ages for the food to arrive, we filled our stomachs by eating lots of butter, piling it on our bread without fear. Later we found out butter is more harmful to our body than lard.

It has been proven by medical studies that lard is high in monounsaturated fat which is needed for health. Most of it is oleic acid, the same healthy substance found in olive oil.

People who shy away from lard probably have never washed dishes. If they wash them like I do, they will be surprised that it is much easier to wash off than vegetable oil.

In all the places I have travelled people eat scratchings. They are called "Chicharrónes" in Latin countries. In Quebec, they are called "Oreilles de Christ" or "Christ's Ear". If you land yourself in a village bar in France, the bartender would give you "Graton". In Yugoslavia, they give you "Čvarci". I love the Italians, they turn the whole piece of pure lard into salami! In regions of the Mekong river, the northern Thai people could not live without Khaep Mu: glutinous rice and pork rind.

I called my restaurant "Viva la Cholesterol".

Lovers of lard gather there. It is still going thirty years on.

With respect to people who do not eat pork for their religious beliefs, I love lard.

THE APPRECIATION OF CHINESE POETRY

Chinese poetry comes in many forms. A common one is called Jueju. It is a quatrain a group of four lines. The first, second and the fourth lines end in rhyme, for example:

The mountains of Lou look like a razor from the side,
Far away and near they look different depending on the sight,
I will never know the faces of the Lou Mountains,
But I long to live inside.

There is another one that goes like this:
I am always drunk and sleepy,
Spring is ending and I must search for higher knowledge to be happy,
I went past a monastery and met a monk who taught me,
Now I live my life gaily.

This poem can also be read in reverse:
Now I live my life gaily,
I went past a monastery and met a monk who taught me,
Spring is ending and I must search for higher knowledge to be happy,
I am always drunk and sleepy.

There is also a type of Zen poetry that uses the same first and last lines:
The mountains of Lou and the tides of the Zhejiang river,
You hate yourself that you have not seen them ever,
Now that you have seen them all,

The mountains of Lou and the tides of the Zhejiang river.①

THE APPRECIATION OF CHINESE PAINTING

Chinese paintings are never realistic. They are idealistic and the subject matter is always the same! Same mountains, same trees, same rivers, and they can be rather boring. There are always vertical rectangles, never square and never horizontal. The point is to practice drawing each object differently and to memorise them. When you compose a painting, you put them all together in the rectangle according to how you idealise it. Not according to how you see them with your eyes, but how you visualise them in your mind. There is always a blank space at the top, letting your imagination run wild and this is where your journey to infinity begins.

Ok, let us walk into a Chinese painting. First, you see a river, then there is a boat.There are two figures who have just reached the shore. One is a scholar, which is yourself, the other is a boy servant who carries a bundle for you.

The figures are very small, just to show how high the mountains are and how deep the forest is. As you climb up the mountain path you admire how each tree is different from the other.

The colour of the leaves tells you the season you are in. As you keep on climbing you see a waterfall. Seeing the water is cool and clear, you sit on a

① The mountains of Lou and the tides of the Zhejiang river in China have been recognised for thier beauty since time immemorial.

rock for a rest. Without asking, the boy takes out a little stove, some charcoal, and a clay pot to prepare tea. After a few cups, you begin your journey again.

Perhaps there is a mansion along the way, which is most likely to be a house full of beautiful courtesans. You are entertained by them. How pleasurable for a scholar like you to be with ladies who are taught music, poetry and dancing, something your own wife lacks. Wine is consumed and slightly drunk, you journey to the mountain top.

There amid a sea of clouds you see a gigantic red-crowned crane. The scholar climbs onto it and flies to infinity.

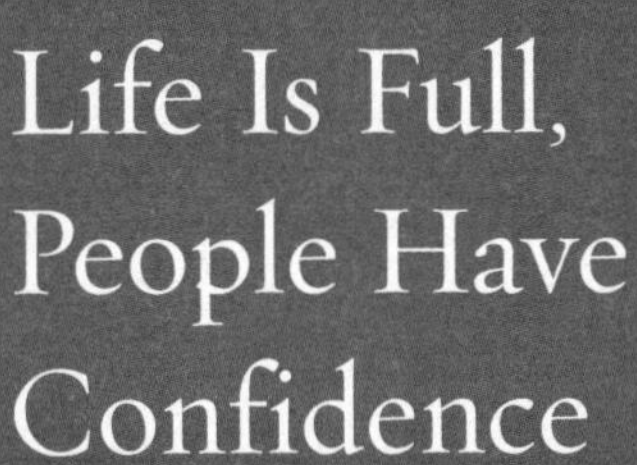

Life Is Full, People Have Confidence

LESSONS

When you travel you learn lessons.

When I was filming in the jungle of India, we found that most of the people there were vegetarian. As we were foreign guests, we were occasionally treated with chicken but never fish.

Three months had passed without any fish and I was longing for it.

"Can you cook me some fish?" I asked the old lady who did the catering.

"What is fish?" she asked.

"Fish is the most delicious thing in the world!" I took out a piece of paper and drew a fish on it.

"What a loss if you haven't eaten one," I gave her a pitying look.

"But Sir," she said, "how can it be a loss if you have never eaten one in the first place?"

When I was filming in Ibiza. I went for a walk on the beach. The water was so clear you could see the fish swimming.

I saw an aged hippie fishing nearby. The fish in front of him were quite small whereas the fish on my side were huge.

"Come over, old man," I said, "there are bigger fish here!"

The old hippie looked up and smiled, "But I am only fishing for breakfast."

THE PARTING

I have been to the Taj Mahal many times. When I visited it years ago, I had to travel five or six hours by car from Bombay to reach there. Nowadays you can fly directly to Agra where the tomb is.

You follow a long line of tourists and slowly you arrive at the gate, which is a huge dome in total darkness. And then Boom! Suddenly you see this gigantic white marble building in front of you. Not only one but two! The other one is the reflection on the water. This leaves such an impression on your mind that it will be difficult to forget.

It was said that the Emperor Shah Jahan built this tomb for his beloved wife and wanted to be buried with her. Not true! If you have time to explore Agra carefully, you will find another unfinished tomb nearby. It is black! The Emperor wanted to build a black marble one for himself.

Anyway, we are not here to give history lessons. You can google it if you like the story.

On my third visit, I stayed from morning till dusk. While I was marvelling at the sunset turning the Taj Mahal completely gold, my guide told me, "If you see it in the full moon it's even more beautiful."

I counted the lunar calendar and it was the 15th.

"I will go for dinner and come back again." I said to my guide.

When I returned, I saw the full moon rising exactly at the back of the Taj Mahal. This made the building translucent.

It was the most impressive sight I have ever seen in my life!

I did not want to leave.

"Although it is beautiful, it is still a tomb. It is unlucky for couples to see the full moon together. They are bound to be separated." I think, if you love someone deeply but for whatever reason you have to go your own way, bring your lover to the Taj Mahal during the full moon, and let the guide tell this story.

He or she will understand and all will be forgiven.

CLUB 240 IN BARCELONA

We arrived in Barcelona with thirty stuntmen from Hong Kong, none of them spoke a word of Spanish. They were all hot-blooded young men and after a while they started to get restless.

"Please help," they said. As a producer and leader of a film crew, I have to solve every problem big and small.

"There are plenty of street walkers at the back of your hotel," I replied.

"But is it safe?"

"How would I know?"

"It still doesn't solve our problems."

I then remembered a man I met on the plane and he had given me his card. It said on it "Club 240 Dos Cuarenta".

I gave it to one of the stuntmen, "This might help."

"It's only a disco," he looked at the card and protested.

"Not quite." I explained that the man who gave me the card was the boss. He said it was also a brothel and all the girls inside could speak English.

"We'll give it a try," they stuntmen said.

"How was it?" I asked when I saw the guys the next day.

"Super! Out of this world. It's a paradise."

They replied looking relaxed.

This aroused my curiosity, "A brothel is a brothel. What is so special about this one?"

The stuntman explained in detail.

"When we arrived by taxi, we saw a line of people, men and women alike queuing to buy tickets. We went in and saw a large crowd dancing. There were many beautiful girls sitting on the couches.

"They were all very friendly so we started to have conversations with them. If you found it too noisy, you could go to another part of the parlour where they played soft Latin music. We saw the man who gave you the card and he recognised us. We asked him why all the ladies there were so beautiful. He said he had bouncers outside to manage quality control."

I laughed.

Stuntman started to tell us more. He said boys meet girls here. They agree on a price and go to the hotel nearby. What an ingenious way to run a brothel! He doesn't have to take care of the girl's medical insurance. He makes money only by charging entrance fees and drinks.

When the girls come back after their brief encounters, they have to pay again to get in. If we go to a disco to chat up girls, we might be rejected. But not in Club 240.

We were treated like knights in shining armour. What a brilliant way to gain confidence!

It is true that there are thousands of ways to do business.

ROAD TO MANDALAY

I have never liked travelling in luxury boats. Those new boats that house over thousands of people. All the rooms are the same. Everybody rushes to the buffet for frozen steaks and sometimes frozen lobsters, nothing is fresh.

The shows are performed by second or third rate entertainers. The game of Bingo would turn you into an old man. You get sick and tired after a few days.

Smaller boats are better, like those which sail through the Greek Islands. Every boat has its own character. The Tahiti cruises are wonderful too. There is one that stops at every place Gauguin visited.

The most memorable boat trip I made was called "Road to Mandalay", an inland river cruise which started from Bagan. It is one of the most luxurious cruises in Burma. The French called their former colonies in Southeast Asia Indochina. The name in itself sounds exotic and poetic.

The moment you board this ship, you would find the river as smooth as silk. One would never get seasick on this tour.

The sunsets pink and the sunrises gold. You wake up every morning to the sound of gongs from the pagodas along the river. Breakfast and meals are feasts of tropical fruits and local specialities.You go ashore to visit many ancient temples, but you could find all this on postcards. What you must experience personally are the people.

First of all you will never meet a beggar like the ones you would see in India and other parts of South East Asia. Why? You will find out later that if one is hungry one can go to any temple in Burma and there you will be fed. The food comes from the common people. Giving food to the monks is the happiest thing in life for the Burmese. Of course, the monks cannot finish all the food and the remainder is shared amongst anyone who needs it.

On pitch dark nights there are programs entertainment too. One of the programmes was called "Surprise". It cannot be performed if there is strong rain or a storm.

If you are lucky, you might see a star coming towards you. Then two, then three, then countless. The sky is full of them. You could not have ever seen so many stars up close in your life. It is psychedelic.

I found out that all the crew members of the boat went upstream in dinghies. There they lit thousands of candles and put these on small floats made of banana leaves. They let them flow down towards us, creating this magical effect.

A mesmerising sight you will never forget.

PUNISHMENT

When shooting a film in Zagreb, we had Sundays off. The local stuntman whom I became good friends with asked, "Why not come to Vienna with me? I can drive you there."

"Vienna? I have always wanted to go there. I have heard so many stories about this capital of music."

"Let's go then," he urged.

"But we only have one day off, how far is it from here?"

"Only four hours by car. The way we stuntmen drive we might make it in three. We can start early and be back the same evening."

His suggestion sounded tempting and I agreed.

On Sunday he came to pick me up. He brought along his wife.

"Turn left! Turn right!..." I found out she was a backseat driver. Not only that, she was also a compulsive talkers speaking non-stop all the way.

I closed my eyes to sleep.

Suddenly I was woken by a siren from a police motorcycle.

The stuntman stopped his car on the sidewalk. His wife started to yell at him,"I told you not to drive this fast! Look what kind of trouble you have got us into... !"

The policeman came forward. The wife continued to complain.

"You never listen to me. It's always you, you, you! Do you know how much fine we will have to pay?..."

"May I know the relationship between you and this lady?" the policeman asked.

"She's my wife," the stuntman answered.

"For how many years?"

"Twenty."

The policeman closed his ticket book. He gave the stuntman a salute and said, "You are free to go, Sir. You have been punished enough."

HAPPIEST COUNTRY IN THE WORLD?

The friends with whom I often travel are "Aman Junkies", so named because they are in love with this hotel group and have vowed to stay in every one of them.

Where else could you find more "Amans" than in Bhutan?

In a survey by the United Nations, the Bhutanese people are the happiest in the world. In quest of Utopia, we flew from Hong Kong via Bangkok, stopping in Dhaka for a refuel and finally landed in Paro.

The air was not as thin as people said. We had no problem breathing in this high mountain country. It was car sickness one should worry about, as all the roads were winding and bumpy. The only flat road in Bhutan must be the runway at the airport. The first Aman we stayed in was in Thimphu, the capital of Bhutan. The guide said it was half an hour's journey, but it took two hours to get there.

All Amans in Bhutan have one thing in common which is that you can never see the building directly but must walk through a beautiful path up and down hills to get there. All the building materials are natural and found locally. Rugged stones are arranged to form the courtyard. The floors are covered with pinewood cut from the nearby forest. There is a law in Bhutan that for any one tree cut, three must be planted.

The rooms were spacious and the bed soft. There was a big stove on the wall for you to burn as much pinewood as you wanted. A big bathtub was in the centre. Everything was well-equipped except there was no TV or any modern electrical gadget. You never saw these in any Aman. We slept well and, in the morning, the sun shone through the window grilles casting shadows that looked like Sanskrit scriptures. All three meals were included, we could have western, Indian or Thai. The food was nothing to comment on, but we were not there for a Michelin restaurant. The rumours that Bhutan is a dry state are not true.

There were choices of local brandy or whisky in the bar but only the beers were good. The strongest one was called "Twenty-One Thousand".

The next destination was Gangtey. Thinking about the bumpy roads, I asked the guide how many hours it would take. He replied, "Six". That meant at least nine, and it actually took ten.

The view was quite monotonous. The law of planting more trees was not working. Most of the mountains I saw were bare. Gangtey was in a valley. We passed many streams with lots of fish.

You need a license to fish them. The Bhutanese do not encourage taking life, hence they do not eat fish themselves. That night in the hotel, we had frozen fish specially imported from India for tourists.

We moved north to Punakha. The Punakha Aman was rebuilt from an old temple. We had to cross a hanging bridge and then transferred there by golf cart. Same as the one in Gangtey, it had only eight rooms, but they were three times the size.

The most memorable sightseeing spot was the temple Punakha Dzong. It was built in 1635 and had endured many earthquakes and fires.

The temple's Buddha statue was enormous. Thousands of red robed monks were praying together to the sound of gongs and drums. It was soul stirring and for a moment you could feel the existence of Buddha.

After the temple we went for a picnic.

Everything was properly arranged by the Aman. British style baskets with china plates and crystal glasses. The food was very good, if only there had been no flies!

Bhutan is a mountainous country. Where do the ordinary people live? Up on the mountain, of course. As there was no way to get building materials there by lorry, they had to be carried up by labourers. With the arrival of TV showing the good life, people long to live in modern apartments on the flat ground. The property developers rushed in, but they had to abide by one regulation which requiring the doors and windows of all apartments must be in Bhutanese style. This created an unbalanced look, which I thought quite ugly.

We returned to Paro where the airport was. The Paro Aman was deep in the hills. You had to walk a long way to arrive at the entrance. The path leading to it was covered in thick pine needles, making it soft and comfortable to walk on. There I took out the packs of instant noodles and asked the hotel chef to cook them. He tried some and was instantly hooked.

The main reason for going back to Paro was to climb "The Tiger's Nest". You could ride a donkey to one of the hills. But to reach the top, you had to climb two high mountains by yourself. After climbing all the way up and seeing the views, friends may ask, "Was it worth it?" After such hardships, of course you would nod your head and answer, "Yes!".

I met a Bhutanese woman who was walking home and carrying her toddler on her back. She probably had already worked all day in the rice fields. She looked up the hill where her house was. It was still a long climb. The expression on her face was not happiness, but profound helplessness and resignation.

I should have come to Bhutan when I was young. At that age, everything was beautiful.

QUINOA, COCA AND MACHU PICCHU

The midnight flight from Hong Kong to Dubai took eight hours, followed by a four-hour wait for transit and a sixteen-hour flight to São

Paulo, and finally three more hours to Lima, the capital of Peru. It was a long journey.

There were big American hotel chains in the city, but we were not interested. We settled in an elegant hotel in Miraflores.

First things first: Shopping. What else was better than buying Vicuña in Peru? Vicuña is called "The Fibre of the Gods", it is the finest wool in the world, second only to the Shahtoosh which is the wool of the Tibetan antelope. Since Vicuña Shahtoosh is trade banned by the WTO, the best product money could buy. Each year Vicuñas are herded into groups and fed with coca leaves. This is to keep the animals calm and happy whilst they are being sheared.

Why so special? Human hair is 30 microns, and Vicuña's is just 11.7! The longest hair is on the belly, but it is the hair on the neck that is precious. The Italian company Loro Piana, which specialise in high end wool products knew about it a long time ago and did a deal with the Peruvian government. The wool gathered was sent to Italy for processing back in those days, and the final products then would be shared between the two with a small portion sold to the Japanese company Nisikawa.

You will find Vicuña scarves in Lima only one-third the price of Loro Piana!

We went to a restaurant called "Panchita", reputed to be the best in Lima. There I saw everybody holding a dark pink drink. Of course I pointed and ordered the same. It was made from purple corn and some spices mixed with orange juice. Quite good! You must not miss this when you are there. The food was mainly BBQ, one main item there was pork and sweet potato wrapped in banana leaves which was quite tasty.

The next morning, we caught a two-hour flight to Cusco. It was 4,000 meters above sea level and I felt a little dizzy when we landed.

The local guide told me to take some coca. We found a store in the airport with a big signboard that said "Coca", obviously perfectly legal there. The shopkeeper grabbed hold of a handful of dry coca leaves, put them in a mug and then poured hot water into make us tea.

Well, when in Peru, as when in Rome, I drank the coca tea. But it had no effect on me at all.

The next store sold coca tea bags which put me off. I tried chewing raw coca leaves over the next few days, but the results were the same.

Maybe they sold some other tea leaves to the tourists.

Cusco was the ancient capital of the Inca dynasty. The streets were said to have been paved with gold, but the Spanish took it all away.

Most people go to Machu Picchu directly from here but as we had all the time in the world, we stopped at a place called Sacred Valley. One could not imagine such a paradise, filled with exotic flowers at 4,000 meters above sea level. The sky was blue, an overwhelming brilliant blue that took my breathe away.

Women carried souvenirs all the way up to this tall mountain for tourists to buy. You simply could not refuse them. There were hundreds of different kinds of Ponchos. How do you choose just one? Easy. Same as choosing neckties. When you walk into the shop, there are thousands on the racks, and you get confused Choose the first one that catches your eye.

The following morning I woke up hungry. Tons of fruits were laid out on the long table for breakfast. There were many types of passion fruits that I had not seen before. I often think of passion fruits as being sour. Not here, they were sweet as honey.

The main food was of course, the Quinoa. Peruvians have been eating this for centuries. The fields were full of this flowering plant.

Not until the astronauts took Quinoa to space and health enthusiasts made it part of their staple diet did it become expensive.

We got to the railway station. There was a blue train waiting for us. It was operated by the same company that ran the Orient Express.

It still retained the elegance of the golden age of travelling. Linen table cloths,silverware, crystal champagne glasses and all the fine dining experience you could get. The train took us all the way to Machu Picchu.

From the foothills there was still a forty-minute bus trip to go. The road was so winding and dangerous that it reminded me of the Yves Montana movie "The Wages of Fear". We arrived at Machu Picchu's gate. First thing I saw was quite a few tourists vomiting. We took our luggage and anxiously rushed to our destination. Climbing up and down a few hills, the ruins of the whole town were right in front of me. I wondered how those huge stones could be carried up to this remote mountain top and how they were so perfectly lined up. It must have been an alien who taught the Incas! In its glory days there must have been thousands of people living in this city, I reckoned.

"Only 750," the guide seemed to have read my mind. "Only the priests and their families were allowed to live here. The common folks had to climb up every day."

"Why did they choose this mountain?"

"There were many legends, but none was confirmed."

"Maybe to avoid floods?" I could only think of simple answers.

"Interesting theory," the guide said.

That night, the sky was filled with so many stars. I thought of UFOs and invaders.

It was time to leave. We returned to Cusco and to civilisation.

The Hotel Palacio Nazarenas was one of the most impressive lodgings I have ever stayed in. The bed was enormous and the bathroom the size of a modern hotel suite. The floor was heated. I had never slept so peacefully for years.

The next morning, I found out that apart from air conditioning, the hotel pumped oxygen into rooms.

After a hearty breakfast we toured the hotel. There was a private chapel covered with paintings. All the Biblical tales were recorded. I looked at the characters in those paintings and I swore I had seen them before. They were the red, round, fat faces of Botero's work.

Looks like he got there before us...

30 YEAR OLD WHISKY ON THE 1,000,000 YEAR OLD ROCK

From Peru we travelled to in Buenos Aires. The capital of Argentina.

My first impression was that the boulevard was the widest in the world. Ten lanes on each side in the centre of the city. It took a dictator to drive out all the inhabitants to make it.

The capital was reputed to be a little Paris, but the lights were few and the atmosphere gloomy. It was nowhere near as romantic as you might think.

Don't cry for me.

We put up in the Four Seasons Hotel. The local guide said their steak house was the best. The portions were huge all right. Every piece of meat was as large as a Texan T bone steak. The waiter never asked you how you wanted the meat prepared. All of them were well done. Very, very chewy indeed.

The meat itself was good, at least my friends said. I thought if it was good it should be served as the best tartare steak. When I suggested it to the waiter, he looked at me as if I was a barbarian! In the following days we had steak after steak, from the street stalls to the most expensive restaurants. They were all tough as hell.

Forgive my lack of appreciation of the Argentinian steak. If you want steaks with lots of flavour, you should try Peter Luger's dry aged steaks in New York. If you want them soft and tender, you should try the Japanese Sanda wagyu. I say this without prejudice.

One memorable taste I had in Argentina was their national drink Mati. It is made from holly leaves. Everybody drink it from a small bowl like the size of an orange. It is shared among friends, filled and refilled with hot water. The taste was special, and I really enjoyed it.

We had a meal in a famous restaurant called La Brigadas. The wall was covered with the football strips of famous soccer teams.

The head waiter showed off by cutting the big piece of steak not with a knife but a spoon.

While the American tourists in neighbouring tables clapped their hands, I felt the edge of the spoon, and it was the sharpest blade you could find! Their best wine was D.V. Catena and Catena Zapata, all from Malbec.

They were strong like the Hungarian Bull's Blood.

After dinner we went to tango. This is a must for anyone who visits Argentina. But the ballrooms were filled with amateur dancing tourists like us rather than Argentinians.

After the big city we went to El Calafate for the glacier.

The boat went up towards the ice. First you saw one big piece. Then much more. You ended up with one that was as big as an island. And it was blue. Not ordinary blue but dark like navy blue ink. There were hundreds of these blue mountains coming towards us.

The captain stopped the engine. With a long pole, he hooked one large piece of the glacier near him skilfully. Then he chopped it into chunks and put the blocks into whisky glasses. We poured a thirty-year old Scotch into the million-year old ice.

It was one of the most satisfying drinks I have ever had.

If you think this glacier was big, it was nothing compared to the largest one in Perito Moreno. It was 267 square miles in diameter!

Long wooden platforms were built around glacier so you could walk near to see it up close. It was like the sky was ice and the earth ice too.

We took a plane to see the Perito Moreno Glacier from above. It turned out that it was a big river flowing into the sea and there it was met by cold air and became frozen. The glacier we saw from the sky was as small as a grain of wheat.

The last stop of our journey was the Iguazu Falls. We flew over endless jungle much larger than the Amazon. A big river runs through it. At the mouth of the river it narrows to form a number of waterfalls tumbling down the cliff.

"It doesn't look very big," I said.

"Wait until we land," the pilot yelled.

The largest waterfall in the world is Victoria Falls on the border between Zambia and Zimbabwe, followed by Niagara Falls and Iguasu Falls. Iguasu is divided by rocks in between, making Niagara seemingly the second largest. But Iguasu is three time higher than Niagara. It is like a thousand dragons rushing down from heaven. A must to visit before you die.

In the words of Eleanor Roosevelt after she saw Iguasu, "Poor Niagara!"

IN SEARCH OF GAUGUIN

I love Gauguin's paintings and Somerset Maugham's novels. I vowed to visit Tahiti, and one day I did.

I got on board a small ship called "Paul Gauguin" stopping at islands where the painter had been. Tahiti is the biggest island in French Polynesia but the population is only 130,000.

There was nothing much to see except clear blue sea and coconut trees. Not all coconuts taste the same by the way. I have tried them all and found the Thai coconut alone is the best.

Breadfruit trees grow everywhere. The fruits are as big as a basketball. The locals cut them into pieces and fry them in coconut oil or ground them into flour for baking. Some say it tastes like potato, but I found it bland. Starch is the main diet. Everybody is chunky like in Gauguin's paintings. I went past a school and found no one skinny.

Some French migrated to the islands, married the local ladies and settled down. They opened French restaurants which are quite good. When you are there you should try the one called "Le Coco's".

I went to the Gauguin museum. All the paintings were replicas, but you could still follow the course of his life there. I bought a piece of cloth printed with the "Two Women" and have been using it as a sarong in summer to this day. Sarongs are not easy to wrap around the waist. You can buy a buckle made from abalone shell to keep it from falling down.

It was time to board the ship and set off to the other islands. The captain gave everybody a bottle of champagne. Whisky and brandy were free to drink as much as you wanted. The meals were "western", no different from French or Italian. If you do not like to eat with other people you can have the 24-hour room service.

There were endless sunrises and sunsets to watch.

We next stopped at Huahine, an island discovered by Captain Cook. The French not only brought their culture to this island, but also their nuclear bomb tests. The island was full of Hibiscus flowers. Everybody had a red one stuck behind their ears. I did the same. There were fish farms everywhere. Gigantic eels were kept as pets rather than for food.

The ship sailed again at midnight.

We arrived at Bora Bora. James Michener famously said: "Everybody who has ever been there wants to go back." Now we were really in the South Pacific. It is most beautiful, and truly a real paradise. No wonder after the Second World War American soldiers came to this island for R&R.

We went to beaches of endless white soft sand for picnics and to "caress" fish. Our sailors threw breadcrumbs into the clear water and a crowd of sharks gathered. Do not worry. We ate their fins, but they never ate our legs.

We could dive in to touch them. They seemed to be happy. After the sharks came the sting rays. Groups of them would surround you. You could flip them over to caress their white tummies. They did not mind.

Back to the ship, you could watch the Green Flash. Few of us had seen it before and it was not photographed. It is an optical illusion. If you look at the setting sun for a while, it forms a deviation in your eyeballs, and the other lights are filtered out,making everything green. I tried it. I saw the sun become a big round piece of jade.

We missed the opportunity to visit Marlon Brando's island. He wrote that when the typhoon came, it blew for seven days and seven nights. If he had died on that island, he would have always been remembered as the captain in "The Mutiny on the Bounty", a young and handsome man not old and fat.

Next, we came to Taha, also known as The Vanilla Island. We learned how to grow the plant. It was so cheap there you wanted to buy tons of it to make gallons of ice cream.

The last island was called Moorea. The main business there was to sell black pearls. I asked a most stupid question: "Why are pearls in other parts of the world white but the Tahitian ones black?"

"Because our oysters are black," came the obvious answer.

It was time to go back home.

Michener was right. I want to come back.

AS TIME GOES BY

If you like movies you will not have missed the classic "Casablanca". It is a name that has been etched on my mind. I got hooked when I was a child and wanted to visit the place ever since. Finally, I was on my way, with the "Aman Junkies".

How did we get there? First, you take a flight to Dubai, then eight hours later you land in Casablanca. Of course, Casa means house and Blanca is white. We saw none of that in this largest city of Morocco. It was old and run-down.

We went straight to "Rick's Café" which had made the town famous. It was said that everything had been reconstructed according to the movie set, but it was actually quite different.

Even the piano where they played "As time Goes By" was not correctly placed. There was no Rick's Café in Casablanca until an American lady who worked in the embassy retired and came up with the idea to recreate it. The news was posted on social media and donations poured in from fans of the movie all over the world. This shrine for movie lovers was completed in 2004 and has been thriving ever since.

Well, the food there was all right, but the dry martini not dry. There was no Humphrey Bogart and no Ingrid Bergman falling into his arms. We had to use our imagination.

The street food was cheap and fun. Hawkers came with a big batch of local bread and the customers tried to choose the biggest one with their fingers. Not for the hygienic,the fainthearted or health-conscious ladies but I did not care. I ordered one, the hawker cut the bread and chopped a hard-boiled egg. Then he added cheese. I thought it was local produce but looking closer, it was the French Laughing Cow.

The best restaurant was called Café Maure. When you walked through the blue door, you could see lines and lines of Tajines, their national kitchenware. Meats and vegetables were slow cooked inside this clay vessel. You could order anything you like. I found the chicken quite tasteless, but the lamb was superb! There was a drink called "Ambassadeur". It was made from sweet dates, almonds and milk. A must to try.

The next day, we flew to Marrakech, a true example of a desert town. I am sure everyone has seen its night market in a documentary, but it is not until you are there that you can feel the vastness of it. There were endless foods and fruits for us to choose from. We had grilled sheep's brain, cow's offal, shellfish we had never seen before. If you think you have a strong stomach, you will be fine. If not, do not even think to try! The best place to eat was a café on a rooftop overlooking a myriad of stalls. Tell the waiter what you like, and he will bring it over to you.

It might be difficult to hold your breath when going in and out of this largest night market in the world. But do try as the pungent smell of faecal waste from the horses and the donkeys might upset you.

Can you imagine growing roses in the desert? Since ancient times Marrakech has been the gem of the desert. Everything prospers and flourishes here. You could throw a date seed and in no time it would grow into a tree. The rose gardens are amazing! and the people there love them.

We stayed in the Amanjena, a resort designed in the desert hut style. The rooms were called "pavilions" and there were thirty-two of them. Two more than the original concept of thirty the maximum. The hotel was surrounded by pools of clear water. What could be more luxurious than water in the desert?

The next day we went shopping. Most of the souvenirs you could get elsewhere, but not the Argan Oil. It is the best oil in the world for anti-aging, said the New York Times. Since they published an article on it everyone has flocked to buy it.

The other thing I bought was a Djellaba. It is a long robe with a hood. After I put it on my friends said I looked like Professor Dumbledore.

The local people smiled at me for my respect for their culture.

The café in the middle of the old town called "Le Jardin" was a good place to have a rest. Dinner was in Al Fassia, a restaurant with a garden full of big yellow roses. Run by an all-woman team, they served us good home cooking. The best choice I thought was a fried dumpling filled with sweetened pigeon meat. I highly recommend that you to try this.

All we needed now in casablanca were the piano and Sam.

THE PEOPLE NOT THE PLACE

If we are talking about Casablanca, then the real white houses could only be found in Greece. There they use a paint that is made from powdered white stone, it does not stain and keeps the walls shining white for years. The roofs are blue to enhance the beauty. This kind of architecture can be found in all the Greek islands making an unforgettable impression.

Our journey started in the capital Athens.

We boarded a ship called Tere Moana because we had enjoyed her sister ship Paul Gauguin when we travelled to Tahiti.

It stopped at all the small islands at which the monster-sized ships could not berth. The hotel where we stayed overlooked The Acropolis. Sunrise and sunset made it more majestic. One never got tired of admiring it.

Although the town are on the top of the hill, we could take a car to go straight up for a closer look. The columns were well preserved. The Greek government spared no expense to restore and clean them to their former glory. It is hard to imagine that it was built in the 6th century BC. No wonder it was copied by the Romans and by the modern Europeans and Americans.

However, it is interesting to observe how the Greeks live now. Every day there are strikes. People get paid even on strike so they are happy to carry on striking. To win votes the political parties give the people extra holidays, citizens now have to work only three and a half days a week. No wonder the government went broke.

To understand Greece, we had to go to the small islands.

The Greeks say that out of all their islands there will be one you are bound to fall in love with and come back. The trouble is, would I be able to remember which one?

We set sail again.

"Is this the Aegean?" I asked ignorantly.

"Good question." The captain said, "It's really part of the Mediterranean Sea. We love to call it the Aegean. It's more romantic. Don't you think so?"

The first island we stopped at was Delos.

Except for the archaeologists nobody lives there anymore. The island is full of ruins of shops, theatres and brothels, the remnants of a once prosperous city. In 300 BC it had sewage systems much more advanced than the third world countries of today.

Among the many islands the most popular was Santorini. The town is on the top of a tall cliff covered with snow! As the ship got closer, we realised "the snow" was actually the white houses with their blue roofs disappearing into the blue sky.

We arrived at the peak by car and saw many churches. They belong to the Greek Orthodox Church. The one at the top had three lines of bells. First line one bell, second three, third five. Rather than climbing all the steps, you could go uphill on a donkey. They had a badge hanging around their necks saying "Taxi".

From the top you can see villas with blue swimming pools, restaurants, and shops. There was a windmill too but with only the skeleton left.

Yet the most characteristic thing was the cats. I have never seen so many anywhere else. Everybody took photos of them. There were countless picture books about these cats.

We went back to the ship to drink "ouzo", the most popular local alcohol. With fresh cashews, walnuts, pine nuts and pistachios, any drink would taste good.

It is often the people you meet that leave a deeper impression than the sightseeing.

Our guide in Paros was not a local but from Germany. She must have been in her fifties and looked a little bit like Vanessa Redgrave. She came to this island some years ago and stayed. Rather than telling us history and geography, she pointed to a church. "Do you see the convent not far from it? Legend has it that there was a tunnel in between. We don't know who contributed most in the digging. It was the nuns I am sure."

"There are so many islands in Greece. Why did you choose this one to stay?" I asked her.

"I like the tradition here," she replied. "When people die, the body is buried for three years. Then it is dug up and washed clean with wine. It is then put in a box to live with the family."

She treated us to lunch at her house which had no electricity. She used a certain wood to grill certain meat.

"I am sure you can tell the difference," she said.

Indeed I could.

When she heard that I was a part time writer, she told me to come back to this island someday. "The house on the hill used to be a local hotel. Since everybody goes to the big American chains now, no more guests are willing to stay there. The government has made it into lodgings for writers. If they write one or two articles on this island, they can stay for free."

This made me fall in love with Paros and I must go back to write a book.

PINK GATE OF INDIANA JONES

I broke my leg before travelling to Egypt.

I had been there many times and there was nothing more I could explore. Maybe I will go again when the new museum is completed.

From there I had to fly another four hours to arrive at Amman, the capital of Jordan. When we were children, before the movie started, the cinema would show the Pathe Newsreels. Whenever we saw Prince Charles imitating his father, walking with his hands behind his back, we would see the young king of Jordan too since then the country was a British colony then. Now they are both old men.

The King had a tougher job than Prince Charles though. There was no oil in Jordan. He had the constant threats from Iraq and must stay friendly with Israel. Under his clever leadership the people of Jordan became the elite of Middle East.

It took six hours by car to get to Petra. With the broken leg, I was supposed to hire a horse wagon, but the winding and rocky path might have thrown me out, so I chose to hobble on.

The walk was actually quite easy, all the way downhill and BOOM! The gigantic gate was right in front of you, all PINK in its full glory! No matter how many times you have seen it in the movies or documentaries the impact is not the same.

The Rose Gate was carved by artists in praise of harvest.

Not far from Petra is the famous Dead Sea. One can really float! Good for a man with a lame leg! Just be careful not to let the water get in your eyes. It stings like hell.

Jordan was the safest place for tourists to visit the many biblical sites. I saw most of the tourists were Americans and they all looked like Woody Allen.

AURORA IS NOT GREEN

We wanted to see the northern lights. Where else better than Iceland?

My friend Mr. Liu had a private jet. We flew to Urumchi. From there to Helsinki for a refuel, then directly to Reykjavik, the capital of Iceland.

Looking down from the plane, everything was white. Reykjavik was a little town filled with colourful cottages like Lego houses. We moved to a wooden hut style hotel specially built to watch the lights. Everybody brought their expensive tripods, their tele-lenses, their Hasselblad and their Leicas. Compared to all that, my iPhone looked humble.

The best beer was called "Gull", and the food was nothing to write home about except for the Puffin meat, which I had not tried before. I found out later that it was nothing to write home either.

"The weather is clear tonight," the manager of the hotel said. "We have a great opportunity to see the lights!"

"I don't think we will be that lucky," another guest said. "Last time in Finland we waited for three nights without even a star!" And he was right, we did not see anything.

But on the second night a miracle did happen.

The manager announced, "Lights! Lights! Lights!" like a submarine captain yelling "Dive! Dive!Dive!"

Everybody rushed out into the coldest of nights with their gear, so excited that it felt like summer. We saw no colourful Aurora, but patches of moving white lights. All photographers were snapping and it was only through the lens that the aurora looked green.

But we kept quiet. After all, we had come all the way here and we could not disappoint the others back home!

WRITER'S LUCK

I started writing when I was in secondary school. At fifteen my first story was published in the local newspaper. The pay was not much, but enough for me to treat my schoolmates to drinks in the bar. Nobody cared how old you were as long as you paid the bill.

Years later I got into the movie business and had forgotten all about writing.

One evening when I was having dinner with a group of friends, I told them about my experiences travelling. The stories were funny, and everybody laughed.

Among them was the chief editor of The Oriental Daily, a major newspaper in Hong Kong.

"Why don't you write the stories down?" he said.

"I can't. I have forgotten how to write."

"Nonsense! if you can tell a story you can write. Just put it down on paper, that's all. Forget about technique. Tell your story as plain as you told us," he advised.

This sparked off my career as a writer, but mind you, I worked hard. The stories I told were well received and readers were hungry for more. At one time I was writing two columns for two daily newspapers and many articles for weekly magazines.

Eventually the stories were compiled into books. The royalties were pathetic but who cares. The articles had been paid for by the newspapers and magazines in the first place anyway.

Years passed.

The number of books increased gradually. All of them were illustrated by my good friend Meilo So. We have enjoyed a beautiful friendship for over thirty years which is some sort of a miracle.

One day at Golden Harvest Studios, Raymond Chow the boss walked into my office. He saw my books on the shelf and said in a sour tone, "If you were born in Japan, you would have earned so much that you don't have to work in the movie industry anymore." He sounded as if I wasn't attentive to my work.

"It's true," I replied, "but if I was born in Cambodia, I would have been sent to the Killing Fields."

IS IT TRUE?

When I started writing, I frequent by received letters from my readers. Some of them asked, "Is the story you told true?"

I remember when I was a child, I often went to a big pine tree near the river in the evening. There sat an old man telling stories to all the folks around him. He struck a match, not to smoke but to light a stick of incense. Then he started to tell his stories from ancient to modern times, from east to west, all fascinating.

When the incense burnt out his skinny little son would take out a bowl and collect money from the listeners. Some gave a penny, some did not. He did not care, but kept on telling his stories. I was captivated and used to sit there for hours.

One evening when it was getting late, he packed up and left with his son.

I went up to him and pointed out that some of the characters in the story were from different dynasties. The old man caressed my head and said, "Son, it only matters that the stories are well told or not. It does not matter if the stories are true or not."

THE FALL

The eighties were the golden age of the Hong Kong movie industry. We managed to conquer the Japanese market and the rest of the world including the African continent with the Jackie Chan films.

I was the head of production for Golden Harvest when the boss Raymond Chow called me from his office.

"Get Jackie out of town. We have been tipped off that a Vietnamese gangster group is going to kidnap him to make a movie."

"Where to?" I asked.

"Anywhere," he said, "Now!"

I had always enjoyed travelling for my own pleasure and the first city I thought of was Barcelona, home to Picasso, Miro, Dali and Gaudi.

Jackie, Samo Hung, scenario writer Chan Kin Sum and I,boarded a midnight flight to the city. We stayed at the Victoria Hotel apartments where we could sleep and cook for ourselves. It was there that we came up with a story from scratch and went on to make the 1984 film "Wheels on Meals", which enjoyed huge commercial success.

From then on, Jackie fell in love with shooting films in exotic locations and our next project was "Armour of God" 1986 which we shot in former Yugoslavia, now Croatia.

I brought a team of 100 production crew from Hong Kong and began filming.

We were three weeks into the production when Jackie had to make a publicity trip to Tokyo for his previous film. It took him five days to fly there and back without any rest. Nonetheless, Jackie was full of energy and started filming immediately he landed in Yugoslavia.

The location was a ruin about 40 minutes drive from Zagreb. There were two walls with a tree in between them. Jackie had to jump from one wall, do a somersault, grab the branch and swing to the other wall. The tree was about 40 feet tall and the ground below was full of rocks. The problem was we could not cover the ground with carton boxes for safety because of the camera angle.

"Can you do it?" we asked.

"Piece of cake!" Jackie answered. "I have jumped on much higher ground."

Of course, compared to "Project A", a film where he had to jump down from a seven-storey building, it was nothing.

The camera rolled.

Jackie jumped from one wall, did a somersault, grabbed the tree branch, and landed safely on the other side. Everyone clapped their hands, but Jackie was not satisfied.

"Let's do another!"

(That became his signature phrase ever since he starred in "Dragon Lord", a 1982 movie in which Jackie kicked the shuttlecock, it was "NG (No

Good)!" for 2899 takes.)

The scene went better but Jackie said the scene was supposed to show that.

"Let's do another!" he commanded.

On the 3rd take he leaped onto the tree from the ledge, but the branch he grabbed snapped, sending him plummeting towards the ground. A loud cracking sound was heard, and everyone rushed to the spot.

Jackie appeared fine at first but as we lifted him up blood began pouring out of his left ear like water from a tap.

We tried covering his wound with our hands. There was an emergency nurse on the set who came running with cotton wool.

"How was it?" Jackie was conscious but spoke in a soft voice.

"It's only a cut in the ear," the makeup artist lied to him.

"Is it painful? Is it painful?" cried Papa Chan, Jackie's father who was constantly on the set.

Jackie shook his head and more blood streamed out and he started to lose consciousness.

"Don't let him sleep! He has to stay awake!" cried the stunt team who had a lot of experience with injuries.

Ten of us carried him through a narrow road leading to a waiting Jeep. The bumpy ride to the local hospital caused more bleeding from his ear and the cotton wool swabs were soaked. Papa Chan kissed his son. Jackie stayed conscious for the whole journey, but his voice became weaker, and he said he felt like vomiting.

It seemed like a lifetime before we arrived at the hospital. But could you even call it a hospital? It was so old and tattered.

Jackie was rushed into the emergency room where he was given four shots of tetanus. But the flow of blood couldn't be stopped.

"We will have to transfer him to a specialist hospital," the doctor declared.

Again, this proved to be another tattered hospital. We even found black spots of blood spattered on the ceiling. I asked the male attendant what happened, and he answered in a matter of fact manner, "Oh, that was a patient pulling out the tube from his own throat."

My stomach turned.

After a long wait, the specialist appeared.

He was a shabby looking guy with untidy grey hair smoking cigarettes one after another and his white robe looked like it needed washing. He pushed Jackie into the operating room for an X-ray.

While waiting we managed to call Hong Kong and were told we had to try to contact the best neurologist in Europe and then the line was cut off.

Looking around we found the medical equipment in the emergency room was actually quite advanced, different from the general wards.

A group of four doctors gathered to discuss the case.

"The patient has a four-inch crack in the skull," one of the doctors declared in perfect English.

"Is his life in danger?" we all asked.

"It is lucky that the blood has been flowing out from his ear," the doctor said. "If he had been bleeding from the brain he might well be in a coma by now."

"What's next?" we asked.

"He has to be operated on immediately!" the grey-haired doctor said.

"There is a piece of bone close to puncturing the brain,we must take it out!"

When we heard that Jackie had to undergo an operation in this hospital, we started to worry again.

"If we don't do it now the blood will coagulate in the ear and the patient will be deaf, which is a small matter. If the piece of bone harms the brain, it will be much worse." He shook the ash off his cigarette again.

What should we do? What should we do? We couldn't make a decision for Papa Chan.

Just then the phone rang, it was an international call from Hong Kong.

"The surgeon in Paris recommends you see the best specialist in Yugoslavia, a man called Dr Paterson, and he should operate on Jackie immediately."

"But where is Dr Paterson? Where can we find him?"

The chain-smoking, grey, messy-haired doctor smiled, "I AM Dr PATERSON."

Papa Chan signed the documents and Dr Paterson comforted him, "Don't worry, it is no different from operating on arms and legs. It is only because the injury is in the skull that it sounds more dangerous." He put out his cigarette and pushed Jackie into the operating room.

Hours passed and another team of doctors and nurses were waiting outside to take over, they were all chain-smokers too. The waiting area looked like the clouds in deep mountains!

Out came Dr Paterson. We rushed towards him, thinking the operation was completed, but Dr Paterson gestured for us to wait. He patted his empty pockets, then asked the nurse for another cigarette. He lit it and drew heavily on it before returning to operate. For God's sake! This would put the proverbial smoking chimney to shame!!

Another hour passed and the whole team came out.

Everybody jumped to their feet, "How was it?".

Dr Paterson shook his head, we jumped again.

"I have never seen such a patient! His blood pressure never dropped during the whole operation. What a super-human being!"

"Is he alright?" we yelled.

"Yes," he said, "but we have to observe him for a while to make sure no other issues develop."

What a relief!

Dr Paterson began smoking again, "It's no use waiting here, the patient will have to sleep. He will be as good as new in ten days."

Only a few people were allowed to visit him the next day and Jackie continued to sleep. On the third day he started to complain about headaches. The doctor told the nurse to administer pain medications, but Jackie hated injections more than anything.

There were eight nurses taking care of him in turn, but Jackie was only comfortable with one of them. Jackie said she gave injections with her heart, but we all knew she had a big nose which Jackie was partial to!

After a few more days, Jackie started to tell jokes.

He said that the pain was nothing compared to the two tubes that were inserted into his penis and arse, which made any movement really painful!

Alan Tam, his co-star, came to visit him. He whistled the theme song to "Friends" and Jackie sang along.

Another week passed and Jackie recovered fast. After a time, the nurses began to attend to his wound. It took them several attempts to remove all the stitches and we never did find out how many stitches there were in total.

"You can now be discharged." Dr Paterson finally declared.

Three weeks later, Jackie was back to the jumping wall scene. He did it beautifully, but even so, he turned to the crew and said, "Let's do it again."

EPILOGUE

When Jackie was recovering in his hotel room, he asked me if I would thank the eight nurses who had taken such good care of him by entertaining them for an evening. Along with Papa Chan and the stuntmen we ordered a big dinner for all the ladies.

The nurses arrived made up to the nines and quite unrecognisable out of their white uniforms. After a four-course meal we ended up in the bar.

The ladies ordered Slivovitz, a local strong drink with a very high percentage of alcohol. "One meter!" they said to the bartender. One meter? And not one shot? We thought we had misheard. No, no! The bartender poured the Slivovitz into special small bottles and lined them up until they measured one meter in length. The ladies took the first bottle and downed it in one gulp, then number two, three and four until the very last. Meter after meter was consumed by the giggling nurses. Then they pulled us up to the dance floor to dance to the disco music. On and on we danced until the stuntmen and I collapsed exhausted.

The last man standing and who managed to keep dancing till the morning was Papa Chan!

Now we knew where Jackie got his genes from.

BUDAPEST MY LOVE

After Jackie Chan was sent to the American Hospital to recover from his wounds, the filming stopped. Everybody was sent home. I stayed behind to take care of the remaining problems.

Then, I took the opportunity to travel to Eastern Europe. It had always been my dream to visit countries like Poland, Romania, Czechoslovakia, and Bulgaria where Dracula is said to have originated. From Zagreb I went to Vienna. There was a highway so straight you could drive for hours without finding any curve.

I arrived in Budapest at night and fell in love with it immediately. All the monuments were lit up. In the old days the Austro-Hungarian Empire wanted to rival Paris, they spared no expense to make this city beautiful.

Anton Molnar came to meet me the next morning. He was introduced to me by my childhood friend Richard Wong. Anton is a famous painter in Paris now but he was then still a struggling young artist then. He insisted that I should see his work. We went to an Italian restaurant. On the wall, there was a big photograph of a young naked lady, her vital parts covered with spaghetti in tomato sauce.

"The lady boss here wanted me to do a publicity photo and I asked for fifteen kilos of pasta. This is the result." Anton quipped.

"Clever," I commented.

"Whenever she asks the customers what they want to eat, they always point at the picture and say, 'Her!'"

I laughed. The lady in the photo was very beautiful and looked Chinese.

"Who is she?"

"She's called Janet. Her mother is Vietnamese and her Father French. Do you want to meet her?"

"Sure." I said.

Janet's apartment was in an old four-storey building. With no elevator we had to climb the stairs. The door opened and she appeared.

She looked even more beautiful without makeup. Everything in the apartment was neatly arranged. I saw a red apple on the table. It was carefully nibbled to make a round white ring.

How elegantly she ate even on her own! The bookshelf was full of Milan Kundera, Maugham, Lawrence, Dickens, all Hungarian translations.

As she went to the kitchen to make tea, I asked Anton how I could communicate with her.

"She is very smart. She can understand from your expression and gestures. Of course, if she doesn't like the subject matter, she will just play dumb."

Janet dressed up and we went out for dinner. First we went to Anton's place to fetch his wife Kristina. He lived with his parents in a two-storey house. In order not to disturb them in case he came home late, he built a stairway separately outside. The garden was big. Anton said that at Christmas they would bury bottles of champagne under the snow. Whoever found the wine got to keep them as a present. I met Anton's parents. They were kind people. Kristina was tall and beautiful. I liked Anton's folks all very much. On the way we passed a wine store and bought lots of vodka. We drank straight from the bottle. I bought them dinner in the best restaurant in town. There were countless aperitifs in the wine list and we ordered ten of them. We lined them up and finished the strong alcohol one by one, like Yugoslavians drinking Slivovitz. After this, we ordered bottles of Bull's Blood, the famous Hungarian red wine. When you are young nothing can stop you.

"I feel like dancing. I feel like dancing!" Janet cried.

I thought Anton would take us to some disco, but we ended up in a big hall like a high school basketball court.

A four-man band played rock n'roll to a gathering of young people. Everybody was dancing like crazy. Janet seemed to know all the youngsters and did not have any problem finding partners. Anton and Kristina danced too, and I kept on drinking.

At midnight, the police came and stopped everything. It was still a communist country then and most western styles of gatherings were forbidden.

The loudspeakers were then moved to the open air as people continued to dance.

Windows of the neighbouring house lit up one by one like stars. Suddenly the music stopped again. The police had cut off the electricity.

Everything went silent. Yet nobody wanted to leave. Anton and Kristina stood disappointed. Not Janet, she grabbed the sticks from the drummer and started beating an empty oil tank to the rhythm of a waltz. Someone pulled out a harmonica and played "The Blue Danube". I walked slowly up to Kristina and bowed. We started to dance, so did the rest of the people.

Far away, a violin was heard, then a trumpet, all the neighbours joined in. The trio turned into an orchestra. Waltzes turned to Hungarian Rhapsodies.

We danced till morning. It was time to bid farewell.

We hugged.

"When Hungarians make friends, they make friends for life," Anton said.

"The Chinese too," I echoed.

We kept in touch even after forty years.

THE LOVERS OF CATS AND THE CAT LOVERS

When cats look at you with their big eyes, you do not know what they are thinking. In fact, you do not have to know. Just love them.

When cats want to play with you, they will come and rub their bodies against you. You return the gesture by stroking their backs, then gradually move your fingers to tickle their chins. They will close their eyes and smile in bliss. Yes, you can see them smile. This is very comforting for us humans too.

My younger brother loves cats. He once had thirty of them. He could afford to keep that many because he lived with my Mom and Dad in a two-storey house with a big garden in Singapore.

Where did the thirty cats come from? In the beginning he bought a very expensive male Persian. His shrewd wife suggested that if they bought a female Persian, they could breed kittens for sale. It turned out that the male cat was a little bit homo and took no interest in his girlfriend. When the female Persian was in heat, she went out and threw herself at all the tomcats in the neighbourhood.

Hence mixed breed kittens were born. No pet shops wanted them, so they stayed. Then came the second generation and the third...eventually they became a family of thirty cats.

All the cats came from the same Granny, but they had different characters. Some smart, some dumb. My brother recorded their behaviours and he loved them all. The monthly bill for cat food alone was quite a large sum but he did not mind.

The cats would hang on to the railing of the balcony with their front paws and wait for him to come home from his office. One cat doing that was nothing special but if you had eight cats doing the same thing it was quite an amusing sight.

All the cats had something in common, they loved cleanliness. They would fastidiously comb their fur with their tongues all day long. If you threw them a long object like a cucumber, they were bound to jump up into the air. If they suddenly smelled somebody's feet, they would open their eyes round and make their mouth into an "O" shape. All the cats seemed to respond the same way. My brother also noticed that if the younger couples got together, the older ones would give them their territories and find other corners to settle down in. They never returned to the same spot again.

Not every cat is lovely. I do not like Persians because I find them ugly. Maybe it is because they have a flat face and their eyebrows are wrinkled, which makes their expressions naturally grumpy.

I love the round faced, big headed ones. They look a bit silly and forever cheerful. My father never cared too much about cats, until one of them always squeezed under his feet, making a warm footstool for him.

Once I was making a TV program me in Japan, I came across a cat that was sleeping flat out in the middle of the pavement. No matter how you shook it, pushed it, pulled it, it would not wake up from its slumber. My crew filmed it and posted video on YouTube. It got 300,000 hits! The Japanese called the cat Neko. "Ne" is sleep and "ko" is a child.

The cat's love of sleep might explain why they had to be domesticated, because if not, they would have been eaten to extinction in the wild. Being domesticated has its downside.

The cruellest thing man can do to the cats is to have them castrated. It is so sad to see them being carried out after the operation, with their tongues hanging out, looking profoundly sad and lonely.

"If you like cats so much, why don't you keep one at home?" my friends ask me.

It is a pity that I live in an apartment without a garden. When I see my friend's cats trying to bury their waste with sand on the cement floor, I feel sad. One should never keep cats in apartments.

But there are other ways. My good friend and teacher in acrylic painting Wallace Ting was a cat lover who never kept cats. Whenever the neighbouring cats came to his apartment, he fed them with bacon and ham. All the cats were tired of eating dry cat food. They loved bacon and ham so much that they came to see Wallace every day. Wallace would put on classical music and let the cats sleep on his paintings. After the nap, the cats would go home. They have became his lovers.

WEIBO

My father told me if you want to do something, do it well. It has been my motto in life since. So, some years back when my friend Kinson Loo taught me how to use Weibo, I diligently played with it every day.

In old China, a rich family would hire a learned man to give private lessons to their kids. Nowadays we are not that fortunate any more, so I play this role for young men and women on social media. I would answer questions that the younger generation asked me. Followers or, fans as they are called here, have grown in numbers, I have over ten million of them now. But not everyone is well-behaved.

My good friend Nee Kuang has his own way of dealing with this.

If a young man jumped on him and said, "I want to fuck your mother!"

He would answer, "I am very old. My mother is even older. She would not suit you. You are young. Your mother is my age. She suits me."

I have no such patience. I can't be bothered to argue.

"How can you stop them? Social media is a game. If people are not happy with you, they just curse you," my friend said.

Where there's a will there's a way!

From my many followers I chose one hundred of them who are intelligent and loyal. I invited them to be my bouncers!

Then I set up another account. Any questions and comments must go through my bodyguards, and they keep quality control. People can say whatever they want, but any foul language will be filtered out. Sensible questions are passed on to my personal account. I would then answer them accordingly.

This does not make everyone happy I know. But you have to play by my rules. I knew this restriction would lose some followers, so I devised a way to keep them happy.

One month before the Chinese New Year, I would announce an open house, during which my followers could come into my personal account without my bouncers at the door.

During that period, questions would pour in. Nearly all of them polite and I ignore the bad ones. Everyone is happy.

At the beginning, the questions were long, but I encouraged them to ask shorter ones.

Here are some of the questions:

Q: Do you feel the generation gap?

A: Yes, I am younger!

Q: How do you avoid your parents nagging?

A: Listen to them. Don't do what they say.

Q: How many languages can you read?

A: A dozen. Only the menus in restaurants.

Q: What is your blood type?

A: I've drunk so much brandy, I think my blood type is X.O.

Q: At your age, what's the most painful thing to lose?

A: The loss of innocence.

Q: What are your shortcomings?

A: Drinking, Smoking and Never Exercising.

Q: Did you never think of stopping smoking cigarettes?

A: Yes, I quit smoking cigarettes. I smoke cigars.

Q: What's your advice to young people?

A: Rebel.

Q: What part of a woman's body attracts you most?

A: The brain.

Q: What words have influenced you most?

A: Do. Chances of success are 50/50. Don't do. Zero.

Q: Why do you still have to make money?

A: My spending power is greater than my earning power.

Q: Will you try every kind of meat?

A: If you have tried them, you have the right to say if you like them or not.

Q: How about dog meat?

A: What? You want me to eat Snoopy?

THE WRITER AND I

It is a bit of a miracle that I have been Mr Chua's illustrator for the last thirty years. One drawing a week, sometimes more, with over two hundred book covers and other extras, it must total nearly two thousand illustrations, maybe this should enter the Guinness Book of Records.

However, Mr Chua and I are completely different.

His career is multifaceted, I do just one thing-illustration. He has travelled all over the world and I live in a small community with one single track road and one shop. He enjoys cuisine from around the world, I live on cabbage, eggs and vermicelli.

Some early illustrations I did for Mr Chua were about the joy of drinking beer and in praise of cigars. I never drink and I am allergic to tobacco smoke. He is carelessly generous with money, I carefully read the electricity meter every day.

Perhaps we do need to believe in destiny.

It is normal for a magazine to change illustrators regularly, so every time I completed an illustration for Mr Chua, I thought it would be the last.

Life was still pre-digital in the early 1990s and so the art director of the magazine would drop the article at the end of the day in my letter box as he lived nearby. So I thought my commissions were due to convenience. However one day I met the art director in the street, he told me Mr Chua had said to him at a party, that he felt I "got" his writings.

In those days, my illustrations were done on Mah Jong paper. People used this paper to lay on the table to soften the noise when playing Mah Jong, but I found it cheap and with an agreeable surface for drawing on. It must have been a bit of a headache for the production department to have to find a big enough scanner to scan the picture. One time Paul the designer asked me to reduce the size of the illustrations and I said, "I can't". I could see him rolling his eyes on the phone, "Why can't you? just cut the paper smaller". I ignored him, after all you cannot restrict the expression of an artist!!

Later I moved to Lamma Island, one of the outlying islands of Hong Kong. With the bliss of having a fax machine, I no longer needed to fetch the articles in person. One time, it was well over the deadline and I still had not received the article. I assumed I was dumped. Paul the designer called a day later and said the article had just come in and could I do it in two hours as the magazine was going to be printed that evening. He said, "Mr Chua's father has passed away."

I grabbed some ink and a piece of paper and went to a cafe beside the publishing house. I sat there and drew the quickest illustration I had ever done —Mr Chua wearing black and bowing. A deep sorrow came over me. I was sure a tear dropped on that illustration.

I left for England in 1996. With the distance and Mr Chua's busy schedule, it was time to say goodbye to the weekly article I thought.

But not for Chua Lam! He said he would write a few articles in advance as a stock and somehow persuaded the magazine to pay for a FedEx courier service every week from the UK to Hong Kong. Not only that, I was also given a small pay rise!

In the middle of some sleepless nights I would hear the clicking and humming of a fax coming through, now directly from Mr Chua's desk, or whatever hotel he was staying in. Along with the article there were always some words of greetings. The header of the fax was "Bo Bo Tea Ltd", so we always called him Bobo and he did not mind. When we were on holiday, faxes would still be sent to me via a little stationary shop in a small Italian village, the lady would wave through the window as I walked past and give me yards of fax paper, marvelling at how I could read the squiggles. My drawings did get smaller, now they had to fit a FedEx document envelope.

I remember before we left Hong Kong, Mr Chua treated us to a feast of dim sum in Luk Yu Tea House. He gave me a seal of my Chinese name carved by him, and a large scroll of calligraphy written by him. He also said to my husband, "I would like Meilo to illustrate for me, for the rest of my life." I remember thinking that was the kind of commitment rarely heard and rarely said.

Thank you, Bobo! ①

Meilo So

① Meilo So called Chua Lam Bobo because of the Bobo Tea he produced.

图书在版编目（CIP）数据

命运好好玩：汉、英 / 蔡澜著 . -- 长沙：湖南文艺出版社，2023.4（2025.3 重印）

ISBN 978-7-5726-1083-7

Ⅰ . ①命… Ⅱ . ①蔡… Ⅲ . ①随笔—中国—当代—汉、英 Ⅳ . ① I267.1

中国国家版本馆 CIP 数据核字（2023）第 036303 号

上架建议：畅销 · 文学随笔

MINGYUN HAOHAOWAN：HAN、YING
命运好好玩：汉、英

作　　者：蔡　澜
出 版 人：陈新文
责任编辑：刘雪琳
监　　制：于向勇
策划编辑：王远哲
文字编辑：张妍文
营销编辑：黄璐璐　时宇飞
装帧设计：潘雪琴
封面插图：红花 HONGHUA
内文排版：麦莫瑞
出　　版：湖南文艺出版社
（长沙市雨花区东二环一段 508 号　邮编：410014）
网　　址：www.hnwy.net
印　　刷：河北鹏润印刷有限公司
经　　销：新华书店
开　　本：875 mm × 1230 mm　1/32
字　　数：210 千字
印　　张：8.375
版　　次：2023 年 4 月第 1 版
印　　次：2025 年 3 月第 2 次印刷
书　　号：ISBN 978-7-5726-1083-7
定　　价：48.00 元

若有质量问题，请致电质量监督电话：010-59096394

团购电话：010-59320018